William Bell

William Bell _____ *e,*
Metal Head, _____ *!,*
Death Wind, _____ v-
eral of which _____ ed
in the United States and overseas. He
taught in China for two years, and is
now a high school teacher of English and
history in Orillia, Ontario.

When he isn't writing or teaching, Bell
enjoys camping, jogging, cross-country
skiing, going to movies, plays and musi-
cal performançes, reading and studying.
Although he claims to "especially like
being indolent," it's hard to see where he
finds the time.

FIVE DAYS
OF THE GHOST

WILLIAM BELL
FIVE DAYS OF THE GHOST

Stoddart

A JUNIOR GEMINI BOOK

Published in 1992 by
Stoddart Publishing Co. Limited
34 Lesmill Road
Toronto, Canada
M3B 2T6

First published in quality paperback in 1989 by
Stoddart Publishing Co. Limited

Canadian Cataloguing in Publication Data

Bell, William, 1945-
Five days of the ghost

"Junior gemini"
ISBN 0-7736-7368-7

I. Title.

PS8553.E55F5 1992   jC813'.54   C92-093466-8

Cover design: ArtPlus Limited
Printed and bound in the United States of America

*This book is for anyone
who has lost
someone*

Acknowledgements

Thanks to Don Bastian for support and encouragement; to Megan Bell and Dylan Bell for valuable suggestions; and to Kristin Kay for painstaking assistance in preparing the final manuscript.

W.B.

FIVE DAYS
OF THE GHOST

Chapter 1

Friday Afternoon

"**A** graveyard? You've got to be kidding."

"No, I'm serious."

"At night, I suppose."

"For sure. How did you guess?"

"But what's the *point*, John?"

"No point, Karen. I just want to check it out. There might not even *be* a graveyard there but it's worth a look. Besides, it's something to do. And maybe it'll get you out of this case of The Mopes you've been in for —"

"As if we need something to do. We've got the whole summer ahead of us. School's only been out for a couple of hours."

"But this will start the summer off with a bang — you know?"

"Where'd you hear about this cemetery, anyway?"

"Remember that History project I was working on for the last couple of weeks? The one on local Indian wars and stuff?"

"Yeah, I remember. What a thrill."

"Well, I liked it. Anyway, according to one book I dug out of the library's local history files, there's an old, old graveyard right over there on Chiefs' Island — used to be called Chief Yellowhead's Island — and the Indians have been burying their chiefs there — after they're dead, that is — for who knows how long. Even my history teacher didn't know about it. The librarian had never *heard* of it and she's as old as the *island* is. So I'd like to find it. If it is there I can do another project on it."

My brother could be a real pain sometimes. Just when you were starting to relax, he'd think up some dumb idea, some project, and ruin the whole mood. Just because he was hot on something, he expected everybody in the world to be just as excited as he was.

"So why don't we go now?"

John ticked off his fingers as he spoke. "For one thing, Dad would never let us. He'd ask us where we were going with the rowboat and that would be it. Two, the place is sacred to the Indians, according to the book I told you about. We don't want anyone to see us going there. Three, it's more fun at night. I'm gonna get some more lemonade. Want some, Karen?"

"Yeah, okay."

When I heard the screen door slap shut I turned and looked across the yard to our house. It was two storeys high, made of dark red brick, with a steep roof and sharp pointed gables with wooden spikes sticking up from them. There was fancy carved woodwork in the gables. Mom called it gingerbread.

Some of my friends said our house was creepy, like the ones in novels or the movies, perched like a crow up on the hill and glaring down at people. But I didn't think so. I loved it. It was over a hundred years old and Mom and Dad had worked away at it since I was a baby, fixing it up and modernizing it.

I turned back and laid my head on my forearm. What I really wanted to do that day was stretch out on the dock and soak up some rays like I was doing before John started all that graveyard talk. I had on my brand-new Olympic Gold bathing suit that I had to practically *beg* Mom to buy for me. I was having a good time. School was finally over — I thought I'd never get through grade eight without six heart attacks and a nervous breakdown — and today The Stork let classes out early because it was the last day. So I ran straight home, put on my bathing suit, and flopped on the dock. Soon as John got home — he was in grade nine — we went swimming.

It was nice, lying there, letting the hot sun cook the water beads off my skin. I could feel the rough hot planks under me and the water lapped quietly against the dock's crib. There was a light breeze and it whispered in the big weeping willow that hung over the water. I felt like I could sleep forever.

I raised my head and looked across the green lake. The sun bounced off the surface, making me squint. Chiefs' Island lay out there about a mile off shore, dark and mysterious. I had never been on the island and I didn't know anyone who had. It was part of the Rama Reserve on the other side of the lake and the Indians didn't like people going there. Everybody in Orillia knew that.

Now John wanted to go. At night. To search for a graveyard. Pretty lame, if you ask me, I thought.

I hated to admit it but I was half interested. John was really smart and he'd get so wound up about things, he sort of wound *you* up too. I laid my head on my arms again and closed my eyes. I began to imagine a cemetery at night — the kind you see in horror movies. Lots of old gravestones, leaning and broken, white in the moonlight. Long grass and brambles that hiss and tug at your legs as you walk. Around the graveyard, crooked trees with bare branches. The moon throwing the twisted shadows of the branches onto the gravestones. And in front of each gravestone, a black shadow, like an open well that goes down into the cold ground.

Down to where a dead body lies, the rotting flesh crumbling from white crooked bones. A body that begins to move.

"Here, take this."

With a shriek I jumped to my hands and knees. John was standing beside me, holding out a glass of lemonade.

"Jeeze, John! You scared me to death!"

"Sorry." He looked into the glass. "This lemonade doesn't look scary to me."

"Hah, hah, very funny." I was still shaking. I sat back down on the dock and reached for the frosty glass, trying to keep my hand steady. I took a big long swallow. The sour-sweet lemonade made my throat ache.

John sat down on the end of the dock with his back to me, letting his feet dangle in the water. He was pretty skinny — I could see his ribs, and all the bones in his spine stuck out. Although he was only two years older he was a lot taller than me, with almost-blonde hair. My girlfriends thought

John was cute. They were probably right, except he had about eight pounds of braces in his mouth. A couple of years ago he had to wear one of those metal rings that circle your head and press against the braces on your teeth. After that he had elastics. Every time he smiled it looked like someone had strung a cat's cradle on his teeth. Now he just had the braces.

We got along great. I knew most kids didn't get along with their brothers or sisters, but John and I did. We fought sometimes, naturally, mostly because of his You're Just a Girl attitude. But we were pretty close and we did a lot of things together. I guessed that was why he picked me to tell about the graveyard project. I wished this time he had picked someone else.

"Hey," I said as a new thought popped into my head. Maybe I could get out of this yet. "Why not take that friend of yours — Weird What's-his-name? Isn't he supposed to be *the* expert on graveyards and stuff?"

"Noah."

"Huh?"

"His name is Weird Noah. And he's not my friend — he's just in my class. I hardly know him."

"Oh."

I didn't really believe all that stuff about ghosts and goblins and witches and werewolves. But they scared me anyway. Horror movies gave me the creeps and I spent half the time hiding behind the seat. Especially the movies about vampires. John laughed at them, and at me. He didn't believe in anything he couldn't see or hear or write a report about.

So searching for a forbidden graveyard at night on an island where we weren't supposed to be anyway was just a big laugh to him.

"Well, what about it, Karen? Want to go with me or not?"

I wanted to say no, but I was kind of curious. And like I said, John had a way of getting you wound up about things.

"I don't know. I'll think about it. Mom and Dad will foam at the mouth if they find out."

"They won't find out. We'll leave after they've gone to bed. Besides, we should go after midnight anyway. There'll be a moon tonight."

The ice cubes clinked as he put his empty glass down on the planks. Then he stood and cannon-balled into the lake. He burst to the surface and lay on his back, flapping his arms and barking like a seal.

"What about it, Karen?" he yelled between barks.

"Oh, all right," I answered. "Maybe I'll get lucky and you'll get lost and I can leave you there all summer."

I tried to laugh, but it didn't come out right.

Chapter 2

Friday Afternoon and Evening

A fter I had cooked in the sun and swum a few more times I went into the house. I heard classical music floating from my dad's study so I wandered in there to see what he was up to.

My dad's study was at the front of the house and it looked out across the lawn to the high cedar hedge that hid our house from the street. The study had lots of windows and the walls were covered with shelves crammed with books on all kinds of boring subjects that my dad liked — philosophy, religion, history, poetry. He had a few novels too. He made the shelves himself.

My dad was sitting on his stool, hunched over his big drafting desk. He was a cartoonist, and his cartoons were in a few magazines in Canada and the States. He also wrote picture books for kids. He did all his work at home and just mailed it in. A couple of times a year he had to take a trip for a few days — like the one this coming Sunday. He and Mom were flying to Vancouver in the morning for a few days — some kind of cartoonists' convention. Whatever *that* was. Maybe they all sat around making faces and telling jokes.

I liked having Dad around all the time. Even when I was at school I liked knowing that he was at home, working or doing housework or cooking.

"Hi, Dad," I said.

He turned around. He was wearing shorts and an Orillia YMCA T-shirt. His favourite leather sandals were on his bare feet. He had a stub of a charcoal stick in his hand and his fingers were all black from shading. He liked to work with charcoal even though it was old-fashioned.

In a way, you wouldn't expect a guy like my dad to be an artist. He wasn't a big guy, but he was built like a weight lifter. He had been a wrestler in college and he belonged to the Y near our house and went there twice a week to work out. Sometimes I thought he looked like one of his cartoon characters — a big friendly guy with a round face, red hair cut really short, and freckles all over him.

"Hi, Karen. How was the swim?"

"Great. The water's nice."

I walked over to him and climbed up on his lap — which wasn't easy, because the stool was higher than an ordinary chair. He looped one arm around me and hugged. We talked for awhile about the cartoon series he was working on. It was about a fat little magician who lived hundreds of years ago. He was a great magician but he lived in a cave all the time because he was afraid to come out. He thought that if he did he would lose all his magical powers.

On Dad's drafting table was a big sheet of paper divided into squares. Most of the frames were filled with drawings of the magician.

"You know, you're getting too big to sit on my lap anymore. After all," he smiled, "you're a grade eight grad now, even if you are a year younger than the rest of the kids."

Dad meant that I had skipped a grade a few years ago.

"Once you start going to O.D. you'll be too sophisticated to want hugs."

O.D. was the high school about five blocks up the hill from our house. The letters stand for Orillia District, and that's short for Orillia District Collegiate and Vocational Institute, which according to John is the longest and dumbest name for a high school in Canada. Or the world.

"Are you looking forward to high school?"

I picked up one of the clips he used to hold his paper on the table and turned it over and over in my hand.

"Well . . . sort of."

"What do you mean, 'sort of'? I thought you couldn't wait to get out of Hillcrest."

"I don't know, Dad. It's sort of scary, you know? There's lots more kids at O.D. and I hardly know any of them and I don't know any of the teachers."

"I know what you mean. Don't feel bad about being a little scared. Everybody is. This is a transition in your life, you see? You're maturing."

Yeah, sure, I thought. Except all the girls in my class had their periods and I was still waiting around like the last kid to get picked for sides at a baseball game. At least they all *said* they had theirs. I had been pretending since Christmas. Yet the whole time I was sort of hoping I'd *never* get it.

I tossed the clip back onto the drafting table. It came to rest on the end of the little magician's nose.

"So this summer is sort of a transition between your childhood and your adolescence," Dad went on. "It's just a natural stage in growing up."

I began to pull at the long red hairs on his thick forearm — a habit I'd had since I was . . . well . . . for as long as I could remember.

"Dad, I . . . sometimes, do you ever feel like you don't *want* to grow up?"

He was silent for a moment. "Yup. For me it's a little different, though. I am grown up. But sometimes I wish I could stop the clock. Then I'd have you and John around forever and your mother and I wouldn't get old."

What he said made me feel a little better. But then he started talking again.

"I think maybe part of the way you feel has to do with Kenny, don't you?"

His words made me feel uncomfortable. "What do you mean?"

"Well, I think you still haven't really faced the fact that Kenny's gone. Maybe that's why you don't want to grow up. Because growing up means leaving him behind. Does that make sense?"

I was sorry I had started all this. I wanted it to stop.

"Dad, I think I'll — "

"Karen, you've got to face it sooner or later. It happened almost two years ago."

I jumped down from his lap and ran from the room.

That night after supper I went up to my room on the second floor at the back of the house. The best thing about my room was the big bay window on the east wall. The window looked out past two huge maples and across the yard to the lake. The thick blue curtains were made by my grandmother and they had hung in her bedroom before she got sick and sold her house and moved into Hillcrest Lodge. In front of the window a set of wind chimes hung from the high ceiling.

Even on dull days the room was filled with light, especially since I put my dresser with the mirror on it against the wall opposite the window, beside the closet door. The light would sort of splash off the mirror and back into the room.

My waterbed was on the south wall, opposite the door to the upstairs hall. It was framed in pine and covered — when it was made, that is — with a blue spread. Beside the hall door was my pine desk, with a pottery reading lamp. Between the desk and the bed, a Persian carpet almost covered the hardwood floor.

The walls were covered with old-fashioned flower-patterned wallpaper. Above my desk I had a lot of family pictures hanging in old wooden frames — both sets of grandparents, my Mom and Dad's wedding picture, John, Kenny and me on a pier in Prince Edward Island.

I liked my room and spent a lot of time there, away from everything.

I closed my door and slid the bolt across to lock it. I dragged the chair from my desk to the big walk-in closet, opened the door, and set the chair inside. Climbing onto the chair, I reached up to the shelf and lifted down the secret box.

I carried the box to my desk, put it down, and then dragged the chair back. I went to my waterbed and got down on my knees and reached up under the bed at the corner of the wooden frame. There was a little shelf there where the two pieces of wood fit together. My fingers found the key.

The key fit the big padlock on the box. The box was about a foot and a half square, made of wood, with brass on top of the wood. The brass was all carved up with astrology signs — stars and scorpions and crabs and bears — and right below the lock was a big picture of the Gemini, the twins.

I opened the box and carefully, one by one, lifted out the objects inside. No one in my family knew I had them. A red, white and blue striped rubber ball. On the white stripe the word *Kenny* had been printed backwards in blue ink. A big white plastic toy airplane with a yellow pull-string attached to the nose. When you pulled it along the floor it made a *click, click, click* sound and the pilot's head turned from side to side. The pilot had a blue coat and blue cap. A slingshot made from a coat hanger and thick elastic bands. A gold-coloured pocket watch on a thick chain. There were Roman numerals on the face, but no hands. Two pink plastic skateboard wheels and a chunk of splintered painted wood. Last, a picture. A little boy standing on our dock, holding a string with both hands. He was wearing jeans with holes in the knees and a Hillcrest T-shirt and his ragged running shoes had no laces. His whole body was bent to the side from the weight of the big pike on the end of the string. The little boy had a grin on his face and his eyes sparkled. He had red hair, green eyes, and freckles on his fat cheeks. He was my brother. My twin.

Whenever I took those things out of the box I'd hope that the big empty hole inside me would stop hurting. But it never did.

I put the things back in the box, locked it, and put it back in the hiding place. Then I hid the key. I set my clock radio for 12:00 p.m. and turned the volume to low. Just to be safe, I turned the buzzer to ON.

I changed into my pajamas and got into bed. But I didn't fall asleep for a long time.

Because a picture began to form itself in my mind. I tried to fight it off, but I couldn't. I couldn't. So I gave up, and let the picture grow.

Kenny stood in the pool of cool shade under the branches of the big willow at the foot of our yard. He was holding his new street board by the front truck.

"Karen! Karen! Lookit! I can do a Simon Sez!"

He had on pink running shoes, baggy jammers and a green T-shirt with a big outline of Prince Edward Island on it. His red hair stuck out from under his helmet and his elbow pads were scuffed and dirty. Blood trickled from a scrape on one knee.

I was sitting up on our branch, leaning back against the rough willow trunk, reading. I didn't feel like climbing down and going out the front to watch Kenny do a skateboard trick for the millionth time.

"Not right now, Kenny. I want to finish the last chapter. Then I'll come."

The brightness drained from his face. He turned and burst through the branches, out of the cool cave of the willow.

"I don't give a care!" He tossed the words over his shoulder as he left. "Stupid book!"

I turned the page. I was reading The Lion, the Witch and the Wardrobe and even though The Horse and His Boy was waiting for me up in my room I read very slowly because I didn't want the book to end.

A fishing boat droned by. A bumblebee buzzed in the leaves and a white butterfly fluttered in and out of the branches.

Then the explosion happened. That's the only word I can think of to describe it — a deafening explosion of panic and fear inside my head. I went numb and dropped my book, nearly falling off the branch. I put out my hand to the trunk of the willow for balance.

At the same time I heard tires screech out on the road in front of the house. Then the terror that crashed in my head gave way to sharp, blinding pain and a feeling of . . . confusion.

I struggled down off the branch and stood on the ground, moaning and swaying, holding my head. The pain was horrible.

I pushed through the branches, stumbling and falling on the grass.

"Karen! Karen!" A woman's voice. Hysterical. I knew what was wrong even before I heard her.

I started running and stumbling across the back-yard, past the corner of the house where the woman — it was Mrs. Scott, our neighbour — stood, her hand covering her mouth.

"Kenny!" I shrieked as I ran down the driveway and into the street.

A big black Chev was turned sideways in the middle of the road, surrounded by a lot of people dressed in bathing suits, shorts and T-shirts.

I pushed through the crowd. In front of the black car was a chunk of splintered wood painted in crazy colours. And two pink skateboard wheels, ripped from the trucks, lying in a pool of blood.

Kenny lay on his stomach, his arms caught under him, his head to the side, his blank eyes staring at the stream of blood that flowed from his mouth to the skateboard wheels.

day two

Chapter 3

Early Saturday Morning

Buzz! Buzz! Buzz! Buzz!

I reached over and slapped the top of my clock radio. Ugh! I hated waking up in the middle of the night. Sitting up in bed, I leaned back against the headboard and rubbed the sleep from my eyes.

I climbed out of the waterbed and pulled on my jeans and a flannel shirt, my socks and Nikes. Then I added a wool sweater. It might be cold on the lake at night.

I padded quietly down the hall to John's room and tapped gently on the door. I heard him moving around inside, so I went right in. The only light came from the study lamp on his desk.

John was already dressed — black turtleneck sweater, black jeans, and waterproof black hiking boots — as if it was Halloween and he was going out as a burglar. He was putting some things into a small red nylon pack sack and mumbling to himself like an old man whose memory was falling apart. On his desk top was a row of what he would call "items." I saw a compass, a Swiss Army knife, two small flashlights, a small notebook, a pen, a bottle of bug lotion, two chocolate bars.

"How long will we be on the island?" I asked. "A month?"

"Be prepared, the Boy Scouts say."

John sounded excited. He loved this kind of stuff.

I pointed to the chocolate bars. "Can I have one of those now? I'm starved."

"No way. They're for emergency only."

He put the rest of the items in the pack, one by one. I could imagine him ticking them off the list in his mind. He zipped up the pack and turned to me.

"Ready?"

"As I'll ever be."

"No, you're not. Go put some rubber boots on."

"Boots? What for?"

" 'Cause it rained after supper, that's why. While you were sleeping."

I was glad to hear that. It was an excuse. "I'm not going in the rain," I said.

"It's clear now. With an almost full moon. You'll see."

We slipped down the hall and crept down the narrow back stairs that led from the second floor to the kitchen. Mom told me that a long time ago these stairs were for servants who would have lived in the attic. They could go into the kitchen to work without disturbing the rich people who owned the house.

John was almost right about the weather. The

back yard was moonlit but there were a few shreds of cloud in the sky. I looked out on the lake. There was a black smudge on the horizon — Chiefs' Island.

We slipped out the kitchen door and ran across the wet grass to the boathouse. It was dead dark inside. John pulled the door shut behind us, felt around inside his pack, and got out one of the flashlights.

Soon we were in the rowboat, wearing our life jackets, making our way over the calm water toward the island. I was sitting in front, facing backward, and I could see all the lights of the town. On the left the legion hall was all lit up and the white beacon was flashing on top of the phony lighthouse of the seafood restaurant next door to it. The town dock was dark — a little too early in the season for boats to be passing through. High on the hill I could see the big lit-up cross on top of Guardian Angels Church. A lot of the kids called it the Bingo Cross because of the bingo games in the church basement every weekend.

John kept rowing, pulling us farther and farther away from the lights. I began to feel creepy. There was a thin cool breeze twitching my hair, and up in the sky the moon stared down at us like a sick eye. Around us was dead silence, except for the splash of the oars and the ripple of the little waves off the bow of the boat.

I turned around, surprised to see how close the island loomed. It filled the horizon. I turned back and looked at the lights. They seemed to have faded.

The oars thumped as John rested them on the

gunwales of the boat. He turned to face me.

"Let's put some bug lotion on before we get to shore," he whispered.

After we had rubbed the greasy stuff on our faces, necks and hands, John started rowing again and soon I could hear wavelets washing the shore of the island.

The bow of the rowboat bumped up onto a rocky shelf and I scrambled out. John shipped the oars, grabbed his pack, wobbled to the bow and stepped onto shore. Together we dragged the little boat up onto the rock. As we took off our life jackets and tossed them into the boat I looked back across the dark water to our house, a long way off. Upstairs, one light burned in a window. Mine.

"Maybe we should pull the boat up under the trees to keep it out of sight," John said, looking around. "Don't forget, this island is forbidden ground."

"Come on, John, who's gonna be out on the lake in the middle of the night?"

"I don't know. Fishermen, maybe?" He laughed.

"People don't go fishing at twelve o'clock, dingbat."

"Speaking of time, I'll set my watch for two o'clock. If we don't find anything by then we'll come back."

"No way! One o'clock. I'm not wandering around in the bush at night for two hours!"

"But it's half past twelve, now. That's only half an hour. How about one-thirty? A fair compromise."

Fair, except that one-thirty was probably the time John wanted all along. He slapped at a mosquito and set his electronic watch alarm. Then he dug flashlights out of the pack and handed one to me.

"Don't use this unless you have to. We'll be able to see pretty well once we get used to the dark in the bush."

Then it hit me. We were whispering. Why? There was no one around for miles. I hoped.

John shrugged the pack onto his back. "Okay, let's go."

I didn't ask him if he had a plan. John never did *anything* without a plan. He never forgot his lunch when he was leaving for school, never forgot his homework, never forgot anything. I bet each morning he even planned when he'd go to the *bathroom* that day. Probably wrote it down, too.

Holding his compass, he led the way off the rock shelf that lined the shore and stepped into the trees. Two things happened. It got black dark, and the mosquitoes found us. But in a few minutes my eyes got used to the darkness and the bug lotion kept the mosquitoes off my skin. Most of them.

As we walked along slowly, groping ahead of us, I couldn't get rid of the feeling that we shouldn't have been there. I felt like a thief or a trespasser. I didn't like the dark, either. It was creepy in the bush at night. There were noises. Rustles. Animal sounds. Out on the lake a loon cried, *Aalooooooo, Aalooooooooo*.

"How are we gonna know if we find the cemetery? And how are we gonna find it in the dark?" I whispered to John's back.

He turned to face me and waved away a mosquito, then started to count on his fingers as he talked.

"I'm working back and forth in a zigzag pattern. If it's on this end of the island, which it's supposed to be, we're bound to run across it. It stands to reason that it will be in a clearing. A clearing is easy to find."

When we started moving again I heard something that turned me cold. I stopped dead. So did John.

"A wolf!" I hissed.

The long eerie howl sounded again. It sounded close.

"There haven't been wolves around here for generations, Karen. Come on, get serious."

I wasn't so sure. And John's whisper told me he wasn't as certain as his words were. The howl came again, angry and sad. I suddenly felt colder.

"Dogs," said John. "It's dogs on the other side of the lake. There are dozens of them on the Reserve."

I was thinking of the spooky graveyard I had daydreamed about on the dock that afternoon. Only this time, there was a huge black shape gliding between the headstones. Its long white teeth shone in the moonlight.

"Come on. Let's go."

I followed my brother, more afraid of looking stupid than of getting my throat ripped out by a wolf. I wasn't in the mood for one of his lectures about how girls are more emotional than boys.

After endless trudging through the dark bush, stumbling, getting whacked in the face by branches I couldn't see, and slapping at mosquitoes, I'd had enough. I was hot and sticky and my eyes stung from bug lotion. I stopped.

"That's it. I'm not going a step further."

"I don't think you'll have to. Look."

"Look at what? I can't even see my hand in front of my — "

John stepped aside, pointing ahead like the Ghost of Christmas Yet to Come in *A Christmas Carol*.

Ahead of us the darkness was a couple of shades less dark.

"It's a clearing," John announced. "Let's take a look."

We crept forward slowly, to the edge of the trees.

"Yeah, yeah, this must be it!" he whispered, excited. "Look!" He pointed again.

The clearing looked about twice the size of a tennis court. The ground was uneven, patchy with shadows, and overgrown with brambles and birch saplings that looked like ghostly white sticks in the moonlight. But I could still see the gravestones, leaning crookedly. Looking just like the ones in my daydream.

The night sounds had quit. All I could hear was our breathing.

"Come on," John whispered.

The wolf howl cut through the night like a jagged knife. It was long and painful-sounding. It gave me the creeps.

"John, I don't —"

John grabbed my hand and pulled me out of the trees and into the clearing.

Then we turned at the same time and looked at each other.

"Can you . . . can you feel it?" John stuttered. A cloud of vapour escaped from his mouth as he spoke.

"Yeah, I'm *freezing*!" I shuddered.

I pulled John back into the trees. Our breath clouds disappeared and the warm night air on my cold face made me feel clammy.

"Weird, eh?" said John. He didn't sound so sure of himself now.

"What's going on?"

"Search me. Let's skirt the clearing a little and try again. Probably . . . probably that was just a cool air pocket — you know, like you get in swamps sometimes. They're caused by water and air currents and stuff."

"Yeah, well, this isn't a swamp and there's no water and the air is as still as d— it's just still, that's all. Otherwise, your theory sounds great."

John didn't answer. He started working his way along the border of the clearing, staying in the trees. On my right, the gravestones stood silent, as if they were waiting for something.

John stopped. "Let's try it here."

We stepped out of the trees. And into a freezer. If anything, it was *colder*. I started shivering.

"Well, I'm gonna keep going," John hissed. His face was almost hidden by the clouds of vapour from his breathing.

We walked a few steps forward and stood in front of a white gravestone. It leaned a little to the right. The words were all blurred and impossible to read. But I could read the first two numbers of the date — 1 8.

John had crouched down and was unzipping his pack. His fingers were so cold he fumbled with the zipper.

"What are you *doing*, John? Let's get out of here before we freeze to —"

While I was saying those words I had looked up,

and I was scanning the gravestones. Near the far edge of the graveyard was a clump of birch saplings. Beside it was a gravestone.

My breath caught in my throat.

On the gravestone a man was sitting.

I turned away and dropped to my knees and pressed my hands to my eyes. They felt like slabs of ice.

"No, no, I didn't see anything. I didn't see anything."

"What?" John whispered. He was on his knees too, trying to copy the blurred words on the gravestone into his notebook.

"There's somebody here," I finally managed to say.

"What? Where?" Then, "Cut the nonsense, Karen. First you hear a dog that you think is a wolf and now —"

I punched his arm, knocking the notebook out of his hand.

"Shut up!" I hissed. "Take a peek yourself. Over that way." I pointed over my shoulder with my thumb.

John raised his body slowly until his head was a little higher than the gravestone. I couldn't resist. I turned and looked too.

"See him?" I whispered, my voice shaking.

"Yeah."

The man was perched on the gravestone the way you'd sit on a fence while you were watching a ball game. He seemed to be staring off into the trees. His legs were crossed at the ankles and his hands rested in his lap. He had moccasins on his feet, leather leggings, a leather vest, and a leather headband holding back long black hair.

From his belt hung a little leather bag, easy to see because it sort of *glowed*. He was sort of fat — we could see his pot belly where the vest hung open — and he had a double chin that almost hid a tight necklace of animal teeth.

His face was dark-skinned, oval, with a big flat nose and a wide thin mouth. It was like a scary mask carved out of wood — creased and craggy and harsh.

Then it hit me. It was dark, but I could make out every detail of his appearance, even the bead and quill work on his moccasins.

"Let's get out of here, John. If he catches us here, he'll kill us."

"No, wait. I wonder who he is. A guard, maybe?"

"Who *cares*. Let's *go!*"

"Okay, okay, just wait a —"

Beep beep! Beep beep! Beep beep!

It was John's watch alarm. It had one of those piercing, nerve- splitting sounds you could hear for miles.

"Jeeeze!" John hissed. He fumbled with the watch and the beeping stopped.

The man on the gravestone turned his head very slowly.

And looked right at me.

His eyes were dark and empty, like pits with black fires burning at the bottom. There was some kind of horrible *energy* coming from them, and when he turned them on me, I felt trapped, like an insect wriggling on a pin.

He seemed to stare forever, as if he were looking right through me.

Then he slowly lowered himself from the gravestone.

"Oh, no. No. We're in for it now." I was breathing fast and my heart was pounding. The frost from our breathing made a fog around my head.

And through the fog I could see the man start walking. He took a couple of steps toward us.

I heard scared animal noises and realized they were coming from me.

But the man turned and walked toward the bush, away from us. When he reached the trees he disappeared as if he had stepped behind a curtain.

We stayed crouched behind the gravestone for a few seconds. Then, picking up his notebook, John stood up.

"Whew!" he said, trying to sound brave. "That was close."

"Come on, let's go."

"No way. Not yet. I'm going to take a look."

I knew he'd say that. If there was one characteristic that John had that was bigger than being organized, it was curiosity. I knew I'd never drag him away from there, no matter how cold we were or how terrified we were, until he'd seen what he wanted to see. The best thing to do was give in and try to get it over with as soon as I could.

Stumbling over the uneven ground, we walked slowly toward the gravestone the Indian had been sitting on. It looked brand-new. The printing was clear and John started to copy it into his notebook, moving the pencil slowly with stiff fingers. The wet ground in front of the stone was freshly dug. Not one blade of grass on it, not even a dead leaf, not even a mark. I made sure I didn't step in it.

But there was something.

"Look, John."

I picked up the little leather bag I had seen hanging from the man's belt. It was soft as wool and decorated with quills and hundreds of tiny coloured beads. There was some mud stuck to the bottom. The bag was warm.

"Hey, great," John said. "Put it in your pocket and we'll check it out later."

"Do you think we should? Maybe we should leave it here for him."

"Naw, take it."

I didn't argue. I wanted to get out of there.

John snapped his notebook shut and stuffed it into his windbreaker pocket.

"Okay, let's go," he said, taking his compass from the other pocket. He looked at it and pointed to the trees on the opposite side of the clearing from where the Indian had disappeared. "That way."

By the time we got to the trees we were almost running, but we had to slow to a walk to enter the bush. John went first. As soon as we stepped into the trees it was summer again.

About twenty minutes later we were back at the shore, sweaty, panting, our heads surrounded by clouds of mosquitoes. We dragged the rowboat down the rock ledge and into the water. We quickly put on our life jackets and climbed aboard. I sat in the back this time, facing John, so I wouldn't have to look at the island. John rowed fast, leaving the mosquitoes behind, until Chiefs' Island was a dark shape in the distance. Then he rested the oars on the gunwales and sat hunched over, panting.

"You and your big ideas," I complained.

"What do you mean?" he panted. He gave me

a big dumb smile that showed almost all his braces. "That was great! It was fun. I told you it would be a great caper to start off the summer holidays."

He lifted his pack onto his knees. "Want a chocolate bar? I think we've earned one."

I knew there was no use talking to him, so I sat there chewing on a Three Musketeers, looking at the lights of the town. The Bingo Cross was still hanging brightly above the hill. The easy breeze felt good on my hot face.

I was thinking hard. Because none of what we saw made any sense. I wondered if I should mention what I was thinking to John. But he had probably noticed the same things I had.

"John, did you notice anything strange about that man?"

"Yup." He wasn't panting anymore. "I know exactly what you're going to say." He held up his hand and started ticking off the points on his fingers.

"One, why was it cool in the graveyard and not in the bush?"

"*Cool*? It wasn't cool. It was *freezing*. My toes are still —"

"Quiet, Karen, I'm on a roll, here."

"Roll, my foot. You've only said one —"

"Two," he cut in, "why was he dressed in traditional clothes?"

"And why wasn't he cold? He was half naked."

"Right. Four, why couldn't we see *his* breath? Five, how come he was so easy to *see*? I mean, it was as if there was a light shining on him."

John reached out and took the oar handles again. He had stopped counting. He began to row.

"All of those things have scientific explanations,

of course. We just have to think about them some more.''

John had stopped counting too soon. I guessed he hadn't noticed after all. When the Indian had climbed down from the gravestone and taken two steps toward us, he would have had to step in the fresh earth of the new grave. He had to.

But there had been no footprints.

Chapter 4

Saturday Morning

I woke up about five minutes after I went to bed. At least that's what it *felt* like. But when I crawled to the bottom of the bed and yanked back on the curtains I was drowned in bright yellow sunlight.

Morning. I blinked a few times and checked my clock radio. Seven-thirty. Then I groaned. I knew I would never get to sleep again. Not after the dream I had. But I crawled back under the blanket anyway.

It was one of those dreams that was creepy and crazy at the same time. I saw myself wake up in the middle of the night. I was wearing one of those long flowing nightgowns that all women in the Dracula movies wear. My room was washed in silver moonlight. I glided over to the window and stared out across the lake for a moment. Chiefs' Island shone silver, as if it was lit up. There was a power seeping from the island, like thick black smoke, that held me in a spell.

I slowly picked up the little leather bag from the windowsill, not wanting to, but forced to do it by . . . something. I cupped it in my palm and gently pulled at the drawstrings.

I took out a rubber ball — red, white and blue — and bounced it a couple of times. It made no sound. I tossed it in the air and it disappeared. I slipped my fingers into the neck of the little bag again and lifted out a big white plastic toy airplane. I let go of it and it flew off. Then I took a pocket watch out of the bag, dragging it by the heavy gold chain. The watch had no hands. Even in the dream I wondered how all those things fit into that little bag.

Holding the watch by the chain, I swung it like a pendulum, chanting, "It's time. It's time." But it wasn't my voice. Time for what, I thought.

And that's when I woke up.

I got out of bed for the second time that morning, took off my pajamas, and pulled on my new bathing suit. The only thing that was going to get the cobwebs out of my head was a quick swim. Mom and Dad let us swim alone in the morning as long as we didn't go in above our waists. So far I had never broken the rule, even though I had been tempted a couple of times.

I went down the back stairs and into the kitchen, which is under my room. There's a big window and when we're eating or just having a cup of tea we can look out across the wide lawn, past the weeping willow and the boathouse over the green water. This morning I didn't look.

"Morning, Karen."

My mom was sitting at the table, sipping tea. In

front of her was a small china plate with one piece of dry toast on it.

"Did you sleep all right last night? You look like you were up all night playing tennis." She smiled and took a bite of the toast and dabbed the crumbs from her lips with a cotton napkin.

I rubbed my eyes, trying to squeeze the puffiness away.

"Yeah, I'm okay."

I poured myself some tea and sat down. Like my mother, I drink it clear. I sipped noisily and waited for her to frown. She did. I smiled at her and she smiled back. It was a game we played. My mother hated it when you made noises when you ate.

She was wearing a loose white blouse with a thin gold chain around her neck. She had on pearl earrings with gold barrettes holding her long blonde hair away from her face. My mother wore very little makeup. She looked smashing. That was one of her words. Smashing. I wished for the millionth time in my life that I had inherited her looks and John had taken after Dad. Instead, I was the stocky redhead with the freckles.

Sometimes I wondered why Mom dressed so nice when she spent most of the day wearing one of those long white coats the phony doctors in the TV commercials wear. She was a radiologist over at Soldiers' Memorial Hospital.

My Dad came into the kitchen from the study, carrying a big white coffee mug with *The World's Greatest Dad* written on it in red. He wasn't dressed up at *all*. He had on cut-offs, his leather sandals, and a Puma tank top. His muscles bulged all over the place.

"Morning, Karen."

Dad filled the mug up with coffee from the pot on the back burner. He always had a coffee resting on his drafting table. I thought he had coffee in his veins instead of blood. He leaned against the stove and took a sip. Quietly. He looked lost in thought — probably stuck on his picture book about the fat magician. After a moment he stepped over to the table and gave Mom a kiss. Then he wandered back into the study.

When he had left I said, "Mom, do you believe in ghosts?"

She put the last bit of toast into her mouth and dabbed with the napkin.

"No, I don't think so, dear."

"How come? I mean, a lot of other people do."

She took a sip of her tea, holding the white china cup with both hands so that it seemed to hang between her fingertips.

"I'm a scientist, Karen. All my education has been in the sciences. I've never read a word in my whole life that even *began* to prove the existence of the supernatural."

"Oh," I said. What else could I say?

"Ghosts, miracles — all those things are things some people like or need to believe in. But that doesn't make them real."

She took another sip of tea and put her cup down on the saucer. "I wrote out a menu for you kids for when Dad and I are away. Try to follow it this time."

"It's *John* who won't, Mom. You know what a piglet he is."

Mom laughed. Her laugh is really funny. She always looks so sophisticated and sort of . . . *for-*

mal, but when she laughs she sounds like a ten-year-old girl giggling.

"And," she went on, "I've put some sanitary pads on the top shelf of the medicine cabinet in the bath —"

"*Mom!*" I hissed, shooting a look down the hall towards Dad's study. "Dad —"

"It's best to be prepared," she said. "You never know."

My mom. She thought I couldn't wait to get my first period. I couldn't blame her, I guess. I mean, the girls in my class didn't talk about anything *else*. The whole grade eight year was like a big competition. Girls who hadn't had theirs yet kept their mouths shut — or lied. Girls who had theirs strutted around like queen bees, talking about different brands of pads and pretending everything was so incon*ven*ient. The whole topic bugged me.

"Try not to be so worried, dear. It's part of growing up, becoming a woman. It's —"

"Let's just drop it, okay, Mom?" I said harshly. A little too harshly, I thought. Mom looked hurt.

"All right, all right. There's no need to talk like that."

Mom stood and carried her dishes over to the sink. A few minutes later I kissed her goodbye — she was leaving for work — and took my tea out into the yard. The grass felt cool on my feet, although most of the dampness had already been cooked away by the hot morning sun. I walked out onto the narrow dock, feeling it creak and sway a little under me. I put my tea down on the boards beside the lounge and jumped into the water.

It was cool and it felt great. Most of my friends liked the lake to be warm as a bathtub, but I didn't.

When it was cool it felt clean, and when you jumped in the coldness made you suck in your breath. And when you got out again, your skin tingled. But later in the summer the lake would be like soup and you'd swim all day without feeling refreshed.

I splashed around a little, swimming back and forth in the shallow water, then I got out. The tiredness had not gone away like I'd hoped it would. I sat down in the lounge and picked up my tea. I took a sip. And for the first time that morning, I let myself look at Chiefs' Island.

It lay out there, quiet, a dark green shape on the lighter green water. I could make out the individual branches of some of the taller trees in the centre. I tried to figure out where the graveyard was. I knew it was somewhere on this end of the island. I wished it was on the east end, the end away from our house.

Between me and the island boats went by — a big cabin cruiser plowing foamy white waves in the water. Some speedboats pulling skiers. And as usual, a few sailboats with wildly coloured sails. They seemed to be struggling in the light breeze. Lake Couchiching had a lot of sailboat races because of the winds. That's what John said. The winds swirled around in between the islands, making the sailing tricky. When the wind was strong the lake was dangerous because the waves got big. And the most dangerous place was near Chiefs' Island.

But on sunny calm days like today a lot of people liked to go over to the island in a boat and drop anchor along the north shore and swim from the boat. There was a terrific sand beach there. But nobody anchored too close to the island. And nobody went ashore. Some kids I knew wouldn't even *touch* the shore.

I adjusted my chair and lay back, closing my eyes tight against the sun. I tried to relax. But every time I did, a picture of the graveyard would appear in my mind, like on the TV mystery shows when the guy is developing pictures in his darkroom and you see the photograph slowly appear on the paper in the chemical bath. Like the picture was dissolving, only backwards. Then I'd open my eyes and the sun would practically blind me. I'd squeeze them shut again, seeing blazing yellow stars from the sunlight for a moment. Then the dark would come and the picture of the graveyard washed in moonlight would backwards-dissolve again. The Indian man with the scary face would get off the headstone and glide into the trees and disappear.

Finally I sat up. I struggled out of the lounge and jumped into the water. While I was splashing around, I looked at the island, then turned and looked up to my bedroom window, where the little leather bag rested on the sill. The sunlight glinted on the glass bits in the wind chimes.

When I went back into the house, John was up. He was standing at the sideboard beside the fridge, making a sandwich. I sat down at the table.

John had his bathing suit on and his bones stuck out all over the place through his pale skin. He looked tired, the way I felt.

I watched him building his sandwich. My brother is the weirdest eater in the universe. He put a piece of whole wheat bread on a plate, then spread peanut butter on it the way you'd gob cement on a brick. He fingered two fat dills out of a jar and sliced them onto the peanut butter. The juice from the dills started to sog the bread. John paid no attention. He sliced a tomato onto the dills. Added salt and pepper. Then he took another slice of bread and spread a thin coat of strawberry jam onto it.

"The jam is the secret," he said to me over his shoulder. "You have to get it just right."

After the jam, he slathered on some mayonnaise and upturned the bread onto the tomatoes. He took a knife and sliced the mess into two pieces and brought it to the table.

When he sat down he said, "Well, what do you think?"

"I think you have set a new record in horribleness."

He took a big bite and talked around the mess in his mouth. A glob of jam slid out of the corner of his mouth.

"I don't mean this delicious sandwich. I mean last night. When we got back you refused to talk about it, remember?"

"Yeah, well, I was scared."

"Nothing to be scared of. That guy didn't see us." He took another huge bite of the sandwich. His fingers were wet with pickle juice and tomato juice. "I might even go back. I didn't get much info last night."

"He *did* see us, John!" Sometimes my brother's confidence made me mad. He was so *sure* all the time. "He looked right *at* us when your stupid watch beeped!"

"Lookit, Karen. Be reasonable. You were rattled before we even found the graveyard. You were convinced we heard a wolf, right?"

He didn't wait for me to answer. "So everything

after that was influenced by the fact that you were scared. See? It's basic psychology.''

It's hard to take anyone seriously when he talks with his mouth full and you can see gobs of red and green and brown when he talks, not to mention silver bands. How could someone who is so neat and organized in everything be such a messy eater?

"Being scared doesn't mean I didn't see what I saw, John. You talk like I was a winkie or something.''

John was licking the juice from his fingers. He burped. "We found a cemetery, saw an old Indian in traditional clothing, and that's it. He was probably doing some kind of . . . of Indian thing at that new grave, that's all.''

"Then how come he wasn't cold, like we were? We could see our breath, but not his. And how come he left no footprints in the earth?''

"No footprints?'' He thought for a moment. "That's easy. It was dark. You thought he climbed off the gravestone on our side, but he obviously got off on the other side where the ground wasn't dug up.''

I noticed that he ignored the point about not seeing the Indian's breath.

"I *know* what I saw, John.''

"What did you see, then? A ghost or something?'' He laughed the way you do at school when somebody does something really dumb.

I didn't answer. But I was sure that what we saw wasn't a real human being.

He slurped some tea. "Anyway, let's see what's in that little leather bag. I'll come up to your room in a minute.''

Chapter 5

Late Saturday Morning

While I was changing I could hear John blow-drying his hair in the bathroom.

I put on a light blue cotton blouse and loose-fitting white shorts. Then I slipped into my blue deck shoes. While I was combing my wet hair at the mirror over my dresser John came in wearing white track pants and a baggy blue O.D. T-shirt.

"Where is it?" he asked.

I waved toward the window with my comb, trying to look casual. The truth was that I was dying to open that little leather bag, but I had been too scared to do it myself.

John held it in the palm of his hand. The quill and bead work seemed to glow in the summer sunlight that poured in my window. He held it up by the neck for me to see and pointed to the dried dirt that still clung to the bottom.

"See this, Karen? Doesn't look like supernatural mud to me."

He sat down on the rail of my unmade waterbed

and pulled the drawstrings slowly. I half expected him to reach in with his fingers and pull out a red, white and blue rubber ball.

"Come on and take a look."

I sat on the chair at my desk. "No thanks. I'll sit here. You can give me a report."

John started talking in his I'm Going to Teach You Something voice. "This leather is really soft. It's probably deerskin. You can tell from the light colour."

He hooked his two thumbs inside the neck of the bag and stretched it as wide as he could. Using his thumb and finger as a tweezer he reached inside.

And pulled out a small curved tooth. It was yellowed with age and it looked like it came from a small dog.

He put the tooth down on the sheet beside him.

He stuck his thumb and finger inside again.

And pulled out another tooth, the same colour but sort of square, with roots shaped like fingers.

I realized I had been holding my breath and started breathing normally. This was no big deal, it looked like.

"So far, it's yawn time," John commented.

In went the tweezer, out came a piece of reddish-brown stuff shaped like a small triangle.

"What's *that*?"

"I don't know," he answered, just as the thing slipped from his hand. It floated to the floor. John picked it up again, carefully.

"It might be . . . yes! See the hairs! It's a piece of skin. Wait! It's an *ear*!"

"Ugh. What kind of ear?"

"Must be a small dog or something like that. Or maybe a fox."

He put the ear beside the teeth and shoved his tweezer into the bag one more time.

John gave me a funny look. In his hand he was holding a bone. It was clean and yellowy-white. And very small. My curiosity won out and I got up and stepped over to John to look at it.

"Anything more in there?" I pointed to the bag that still rested in his palm.

John laid the bone down on the sheet, then up-ended the bag. A round gold object plopped onto the bed. It was about the size of a nickel, maybe a little bigger, but not as big as a quarter.

John picked it up and turned it over slowly, so many times I thought he'd gone nutty.

"Well?" I snapped.

"It's a coin."

"Brilliant deduction, Watson!" I burst out. "Let me see it!"

"Wonder if it's gold," John muttered as he handed it over. "Might be worth a lot."

It sure looked like gold. It was really shiny and worn almost smooth. I could make out the remains of a face on one side, but couldn't even tell if it was a man or a woman. The other side was so smooth I could see nothing except two numbers, a one and a seven.

"Look." I showed John the numbers.

"Well," he said, "the coin was minted in Some-thing Seventeen or Seventeen Something."

"Brilliant again," I huffed. "As if I needed you to tell me that."

"I'll bet it was Seventeen Something," he said, ignoring my words. "This coin sure *looks* at least two hundred years old."

"Yeah, it does."

He put the coin on the sheet, then lined up all the objects — two teeth, the piece of skeleton, the ear, and the coin — and laid the bag beside them.

Did they mean anything, I wondered. And if they did, did I want to know? I realized that half of me said Yes and the other half said, Put the junk back in the bag and toss it in the garbage and forget you ever went to Chiefs' Island.

As if he was reading my mind John asked, "Well, what do you want to do with this stuff?"

"I don't know."

"Well, if you don't want it, can I have it? I'd like to go to the library and see if I can find out anything about little skin bags that Indians used to wear around their waists."

I almost said Yes. I looked down at the strange objects on my bed, and suddenly thought, Kenny would have loved all this stuff. I said in a low voice, "No, I think I'll keep it for a while."

On my windowsill I had a big clear glass candy bowl with a lid. I dumped out the comb, barrettes, paperclips and other junk onto my desk and, using a corner of the blanket on my bed, I polished the bowl and lid. Then I carefully laid the deerskin bag, ear, teeth, coin, and bit of skeleton in the bowl. I put on the lid and carried the bowl to the windowsill, putting it down in the middle so it wouldn't get knocked off when I opened or closed the side panes.

"There," I said, and brushed my hands together.

Saturday Evening

That night I had a lot of trouble getting to sleep. I tossed and turned and punched my pillow and smoothed my blanket. I listened to the radio for a while with my earphones on, but that didn't help either. Instead of calming me the way it usually does, the local rock station just bugged me.

Finally I tossed the earphones on the floor and drifted off. I don't know how long I had slept before I came suddenly awake. It must have been the cold that woke me. I was *freezing*. I sat up in bed, pulling my blanket up around my ears. Outside my bay window the moonlight was like silver paint on the leaves. The wind chimes reflected the light and on the windowsill the glass bowl sort of glowed.

I didn't know why, but my stomach was in a tight knot — the way it is when you've got an important test coming up, or you did something wrong and your parents found out and it's time to get punished.

Then I realized I could see my breath.

It couldn't be this cold, I thought. And if it was cold, how come the furnace didn't start up? I decided to get out of bed and wake up Dad and get the heat turned on.

It was the sharp tinkling of the wind chimes that stopped me. I looked up at them, surprised, because I was sure I had shut my window.

My window *was* closed. The chimes were perfectly still, but jangling like mad.

The jangling stopped, and all I could hear was my own breathing. What the heck is going on, I thought.

Then I heard footsteps in the hall outside my room, creaking on the hardwood floor.

And a wave of fear rolled through me. Because I knew they weren't footsteps belonging to Mom or Dad or John. There was someone in the house!

I was too scared to get out of bed. I sat there, tense, staring at my closed door, hoping that the footsteps wouldn't come closer, hoping that the bolt would hold. I heard a sudden laugh, then the sound of someone running, toward the front of the house.

Then dead silence.

Still I stared at the door. I pulled the blanket tighter as my teeth began chattering — from fear or cold, I didn't know which. I wanted to run to my parents' room but I was too terrified to get out of bed. I glanced up at the wind chimes, half expecting them to jangle again, then back to the door.

I felt exhausted, heavy. I lay down again on my side with my legs curled up to my chest. I was beginning to feel a little warmer but I could still see my breath. I lay there, staring at the door.

Footsteps again. Creaking slowly toward my room.

The temperature dropped. I moaned in terror and cowered back until I could feel the wall behind me as the footsteps came even closer.

The footsteps stopped. Then — *Bang! Bang! Bang!* — the door shook in its frame. The clamour kept on without a rest, a constant knocking, like someone on the other side was mad, really mad, and wanted me.

The knocking got louder and louder. The whole wall seemed to vibrate with each deafening bang on the door. I pressed my hands to my ears, thinking I was going crazy. The pounding started to echo inside my skull, like a drum. I tore my eyes from the door when the motionless wind chimes began to jangle again.

My eyes darted to the slide bolt above the knob on the door. It rattled and jumped with each booming blow. I looked at the doorknob, expecting it to begin to turn, slowly, like in all the horror movies.

But the thunderous knocking stopped. The wind chimes fell silent.

I flopped back on the bed, relieved, as if someone had pushed me over. I was breathing fast and a trickle of sweat ran into my eye. How could I be sweating, I thought. It's still freezing in here. But I couldn't see my breath anymore.

I felt the heaviness again, and fell into sleep.

When I opened my eyes, it was still night. Moonlight spilled through my window and across the floor. I was facing the door, and the knob shone a little from the moonlight.

I pushed my blanket down. It was very warm in the room.

"Whew! What a dream," I whispered to myself. "Must have been because I stuffed myself with popcorn before I went to bed."

I had almost convinced myself that it had all been a nightmare when I heard footsteps again.

They crept slowly down the hall toward my room. They sounded different, but I was suddenly just as terrified as before. I cowered against the wall again.

The footsteps stopped at my door.

The doorknob turned slowly. But the bolt held.

"Karen?" John's voice was quiet and scared.

"Jeeze, John! You scared the life out of me." I was so relieved I couldn't get mad at the idiot. I climbed out of bed, slid the bolt back, and headed for the bed again.

John slipped into the room, leaving the door open, and came over to the bed and sat down. Right on my feet.

"Ow! You goof."

"Shhhhhhh! Sorry."

John glanced out into the dark hall, then turned back to me.

His face looked funny. Not ha-ha funny. Strange funny. It wasn't the I've Got Everything under Control brother I was used to. He looked scared and . . . confused. Like something really blew his mind up.

"Did . . . did you hear anything tonight, Karen?"

I was suddenly scared again. "Like what?"

"You did, didn't you?" he said excitedly. "You did hear something. I can tell by your voice."

"I don't know what you're talking about, John. You come in here in the middle of the night and scare me out of my —"

"Okay, I'll tell you what I heard. You tell me if you heard it too. Okay?"

I didn't say anything. I didn't like this at all.

"Footsteps, right? Not yours, not Mom's or Dad's."

He stopped talking, searching my face. Then he went on.

"Running, and . . . and a laugh. Then someone knocking on a door somewhere."

He kept looking straight into my eyes. I still said nothing. I was scared. And mad. I had almost convinced myself that what had happened had been a dream. Now here was my real-life brother telling me he heard everything too. I couldn't kid myself anymore.

"It was my door," I admitted.

John's eyes bugged out. "What? Really? Weren't you scared?"

"No, I was thrilled. I invited whoever it was to come in and play checkers. Of course I was scared, you winkie."

John let out a long breath.

"You left out one thing, John. It was cold. Really cold."

"Yeah, I felt it, too." His eyes grew even larger. "Just like —"

"That's right," I cut in, "just like on Chiefs' Island."

day three

Sunday Morning

John and I didn't sleep the rest of that night. We sat on the bed talking, jumping like terrified cats at every noise in the house, making all kinds of guesses about what had happened.

After he had calmed down, which was just about the time sunlight began to creep in my window, John started ticking off his fingers.

"Okay. So far, we've got two possible explanations. One, someone broke into the house and —"

"Baloney," I cut in. We'd been through all this before. "As if a burglar is going to run around laughing and pounding on doors. And what did he do, bring a portable air conditioner? Why don't you just face it, John? It —"

It was his turn to interrupt. "TWO!" he almost shouted. "There's something, uh, preternatural going on."

"Something *what*?"

I could tell he was starting to feel like his old self again. His Lecturing Voice slipped into gear. Except he didn't look too scholarly with messy blonde hair sticking up in all directions, braces, and green pajamas with bright red stop signs all over them.

"Preternatural. It means, uh, something we don't have any explanation for — yet. Like, science can't help too much."

I thought about what my mom had said the morning before. She was a scientist.

John was still talking. "But someday we will."

"Someday we will what?"

"Have an explanation."

"Preternatural. Sounds like one of those words politicians use."

John ignored me. He usually does when he's lecturing. "*Super*natural means that it's . . . well, like gods and monsters and miracles."

"And ghosts."

He shrugged. Getting him to admit anything was like waiting for paint to dry.

"Yeah, okay, like ghosts."

"Well, John, I'll tell you what I think. What I *know*. We saw a ghost on Chiefs' Island. And last night there was a ghost in this house. And somehow they must be connected."

"Boy, your imagination is really ripping along!"

"Okay, what's *your* explanation?" I was getting sick of talking around in circles.

"I told you. It's preternatural."

"*That's* an explan*ation*?"

John knew he was being stupid. His face told me so, no matter what his mouth said.

"Okay, let's do this scientifically."

I groaned and flopped backwards on the bed.

"We'll ask Mom and Dad if they heard anything last night. Okay?"

I agreed.

"But no leading questions. Agreed?"

"What are you, a lawyer? Get out of here and let me get dressed," I said. "I'll meet you in the kitchen."

When we got downstairs, wearing our bathing suits, Dad was sitting at the table, spooning cream of wheat into his mouth. There was a big steaming bowl of the awful stuff in front of him. He got up at dawn every morning, went for a run, and had a bowl of that sticky white stuff when he got back. Winter or summer, always the same.

"Hi, guys," he said. "Want some?"

I wrinkled my nose. John said, "Not creative enough, Dad." He got the bread out of the bread-box and popped two slices into the toaster. I put the kettle on the stove for more tea. The pot was almost empty.

John made a sandwich out of lettuce, honey, sliced ham and peanut butter and sat down between Dad and me.

"Hey, Dad," he began, "I had a really funny dream last night."

"Oh, tell me about it."

Dad picked up the box of brown sugar and shook it over his bowl. Then he poured more milk in on top of the glue. He stirred the mess around. I suddenly realized where John got his loony eating habits.

John described a phony dream that was pretty close to what happened. Then he said, "It was really real, Dad, you know?"

"Yeah, sometimes dreams seem more real than real life."

John wasn't listening. "When I woke up, it seemed like I was still dreaming. I could hear noises." He stopped chewing. "Dad, did you or Mom hear anything last night?"

"Like what, John?"

"Oh, I don't know." John was doing a terrible job of trying to sound casual. "Like footsteps or someone knocking on a door?"

"Nope, not a thing."

"Did it get cold last night?" I put in. John shot me a dirty look.

Dad laughed. "Cold? The guy on the radio a while ago said last night was twenty-five degrees. Supposed to be hot today too," he added.

John gave me another snarl look. I smiled what I hoped was an I Told You So smile.

"There's something I want to ask you guys, now that we're together," Dad said. "Who's been into my charcoal sticks? I found them scattered all over the drafting board when I went into the study this morning. I also found this."

He reached into the chest pocket of his shirt and took out a piece of paper. He unfolded it and put it down on the table beside his bowl.

On the paper was this:

"I don't get it, Dad," said John, chewing. "What's the big deal? It's just some scribbles." He looked into Dad's face. "Isn't it?"

He looked at me. "Sure. There's no big deal. Except one of you has been at my table, using my stuff, which you're welcome to do, as you know, provided you don't leave a mess."

I knew he was thinking about the time about two years ago, after Kenny died, when I went a little nutty and filled page after page of his drafting paper with crazy charcoal scribbles. I spent the next day in bed, drinking hot milk. Mom stayed home from work and fussed over me all day.

"Don't look at me, Dad," I said. "I haven't touched your stuff."

"Me either," said John.

My Dad got one of those I'm Disappointed in You looks on his face, the kind parents are really good at. I guess he decided not to make an issue out of it, because he just nodded.

"Well, all right. Anyway, how about some lawn mowing today, guys?"

John groaned. "Aw, Dad, can't we do it tomorrow?"

"Nope."

Dad got up and put his empty bowl in the dishwasher. Then he padded off to his study. His leather sandals slapped away down the hall.

"Well?"

"Well what?"

"Are you still going with the ghost theory?"

We had finished mowing and raking the lawns

and had taken a swim to cool off. The yard smelled of fresh cut grass. Now we were lying side by side on the dock, facing the house instead of the lake.

"Yup," I said. "And I've got an idea."

"What?"

"I think we should go talk to Weird Noah."

"No way. What for?"

"Come on, John, you know what for. You told me the guy knows *everything* there *is* to know about ghosts and vampires and miracles and all that stuff."

"He's also a freak."

"You hardly know him. Right?"

"Yeah, I guess," he admitted. "But who needs him?"

"I'm going to visit him right after Mom and Dad leave for Toronto airport. You can come or not come. It doesn't matter."

John raised himself up on his elbows and looked behind us, out over the lake. I knew what he was looking at.

"I'll come," he said. "But not because I agree with this ghost stuff. I *still* say it's —"

"Yeah, I know. Preternatural."

"Karen! John! We're ready to go now!"

"Coming, Mom!"

I heard John answering from the back yard as I left my room and ran downstairs and out the front door.

Our old VW bus stood in the driveway in the shade of one of the big maples. With all the doors open — two front, side slider, trunk — it looked like some kind of crazy bug trying to take off and not quite making it.

Dad loved that bus. It had the original paint design, dark blue below the windows and white above, and at the front the white dropped in a deep V almost to the painted bumper. In the centre of the front panel was a big chrome circle with VW in the centre. Dad did the body work and paint job himself.

He did the inside modern, though — thick carpet, a Pioneer AM/FM stereo digital CD with six speakers, a CB, a compass and a fuzz buster.

Mom hated the old van. She said it looked like a blue and white loaf of bread. "It's noisy in the summer and freezing in the winter," was what she said about it.

Dad always added, "Well, you like old houses and I like old cars."

She'd roll her eyes and they'd both laugh about it.

That day Dad looked gift-wrapped in pressed slacks, polished black shoes, shirt and tie. There was a film of sweat on his forehead and he had his I Hate Packing and Going on Trips look on his face.

Mom looked cool and composed. She wore white leather sandals, a flower print summer dress and a string of pearls. Smashing.

"Minnie won't be over until supper," Mom said after John and I arrived, "so you'll be on your own until then."

"Aw, Mom, couldn't you get someone else?" John complained again.

John hated to have Minnie around. She was a cousin — three hundred and twenty-eighth removed or something — who was nineteen years old and hated the whole universe. Mom and Dad hired her to take care of us because, they said, she needed some positive input in her life, something to feel some achievement from.

John called her Skinny Minnie because she was tall and bony, with a long horse face and the worst case of acne I had ever seen. All she did when she took care of us was watch soap operas and eat, or read trashy Harlequin Romances and eat, or lie on the couch and soak up rock videos and eat, or rent movies from Movie Van and veg out and eat. She would eat anything that didn't eat her first, but she never gained an ounce.

She was grouchy and cynical and criticized everybody and everything. That's what bugged John.

I sort of liked it when she took care of us because she would leave us alone. She didn't care where we were or what we did as long as we didn't get in her hair. We didn't tell Mom or Dad that, of course.

After John made his usual complaint about Skinny Minnie, Mom said, "Let's not get caught in a loop."

Sometimes computer talk slipped into Mom's speech. She meant, Let's not talk around in circles — we've been over all this before.

"Minnie is just fine if you'd give her half a chance. All she —"

"Yeah, yeah, all she needs is a little understanding," John laughed. "Let's not get caught in _that_ loop either."

Mom laughed, too. "_Touché,_" she said. "Anyway, she'll sleep in the guest room above the garage, so she'll have her own TV and she won't be in your way. All right? Now, you two co-operate with her, okay? Promise!" she added when we didn't answer.

We promised, then kissed Mom goodbye. She climbed up into the van, hauling herself up with the handle on the dashboard. She rolled her eyes and shut the door.

Dad rammed the slider closed, then came around to the back and pulled down the trunk lid.

"Okay, guys, guess we're ready. You sure you'll be okay?"

He always worried more than Mom did.

"Come on, Dad, we're practically *ancient*," I answered.

"Oh, yes, forgive me. I keep forgetting about your advanced age and extreme sophistication."

He gave each of us a hug and walked to the front of the van, climbing up behind the wheel. He stuck his head out and looked back.

"See you in four or five days. We'll call you soon as we get to Vancouver."

We both waved as the VW started up and rolled down the driveway, crunching on the gravel. Then it turned onto Bay Street and disappeared behind our hedge.

I didn't feel too hot about my parents going away.

8

Sunday Afternoon

After lunch John and I walked over to Weird Noah's house. He lived on Neywash Street, a block or so up the street from the pizza restaurant. It was sunny and hot so I had on green cotton shorts and a halter top and no socks, just my Nikes. John wore his baggy bathing suit and a tank top. He looked like a piece of spaghetti with shoes.

I didn't know much about Noah. His mother wasn't around, his dad was the Baptist minister, and he lived in the manse — the house that the church owns and lets its minister live in.

I wasn't even sure why he had his nickname. I asked John to fill me in as we crossed Couchiching Park on our way to Noah's.

"He's not really what you'd call weird. He's just different."

"Well," I said, "thanks a lot for clearing *that* up!"

"No, I mean, he's a . . . an individual. A loner. He does things the way he wants. Like his clothes and his hair. He's not too worried about what the other kids think. But he knows more about the occult and ghosts and werewolves and all that stuff than anyone in this town, I'll bet.''

We were crossing the grassy baseball diamond. A few little kids were popping up flies and catching them for practice.

No wonder the other kids figured he was weird, I thought. At Hillcrest just about every girl I knew was paranoid about what the others would say about her. Most of my friends wouldn't even take a breath without making sure they wouldn't get put down for it. You always had to wear what was in. And if you were different they'd put their heads together like ducks and gabble about you. I had to admit I was a little that way myself. The boys may have been the same. I don't know. Probably.

"I heard that his father is really mean," John went on. "He and Noah fight all the time. Noah is really rebellious. And I also heard — don't even *think* about this when we're at Noah's — that his mother ran off a few years ago with his father's assistant minister.''

We reached Jimmy's snack bar — a little white clapboard shack on the corner between the old Co-op feed store and the park — and my mouth started to water when I smelled the french fries. A few kids were sitting around painted metal tables, stuffing their faces with fries and burgs, or leaning against cars, sipping shakes through plastic straws and looking tough.

"Anyway, Noah flunked all his credits in grade nine last year, so I had a few classes with him this year. He's not a bad guy, I guess. I don't know him all that well.''

We walked across the railway tracks, past the feed store, and turned left on Laclie. The pizza restaurant was full, and more delicious smells teased my nose. We turned right on Neywash, walked up-hill a block, and stopped in front of the big brick house where Noah lived.

"What are you going to say to him?"

Once John asked me that I realized I didn't know what to say. But I wasn't going to admit that to my Know-It-All brother.

"You'll see," I answered. "Let's go."

I banged on the door, using the big brass knocker. After a moment the door opened.

"Yes, children?"

The guy standing there was short and stocky, dressed in a black suit with a white minister's collar. He was almost bald and he had a scowl on his long face.

John and I looked at each other. We were both a little bugged at being called children.

I finally managed to say, "Uh, is Noah in?"

The scowl got scowlier. "Yes, come in."

Behind him was a big living room. It had a brick fireplace with a picture above it. About seven women in go-to-church clothes were sitting on the fancy couches and chairs, balancing china tea cups on their laps. There was an empty armchair beside the fireplace with a tea cup resting on one of the arms.

Noah's father closed the door behind us and yelled "NO-AHHHHHH!" up the long staircase. He plastered a smile on his face and walked back into the living room. As he closed the door behind him we heard, "Yes, the spiritual life . . . ."

John and I were left standing in the hallway.

"Wonder what *his* problem is," John said.

A kid appeared at the top of the stairs. It was hard to see him because the light was dim.

"Who's that?" said the voice above us.

"Hi, Noah," said John, "it's John Stone. This is my sister, Karen."

Noah came down the stairs. He was fairly tall and thin. His black hair was buzzed up on the sides and long on the top, so long that it hung down in a wedge that covered half his face and hung a little below his chin. But the half of his face that I could see showed me he was cute. His left ear was pierced three times. He wore two studs and a silver cross that hung on a long chain. He had deep blue eyes, with black, curling lashes and tanned skin. He had on black denim cut-offs and a black T-shirt with white writing on it that said, *Apartheid Sucks*. No wonder his dad fights with him, I thought.

Noah looked at us, a questioning expression on his face. I thought I might as well jump into it. If he decided I was an idiot, well, too bad.

"We're here because we got a problem and you're the only one we know who might be able to help us with it."

He looked at John.

"Yeah, that's about it," John said.

"What kinda problem?" His voice was deep and smooth, an adult's voice.

My courage was beginning to slip a little. I started to feel dumb.

"Um, well, it's sort of about . . . a ghost." I looked down at the toes of my Nikes.

Noah talked like you'd talk if someone had said it might rain tomorrow.

"Yeah? Well, you might as well come up."

He turned and started up the stairs. John and I followed him upstairs, down a dark hall and into a big room. Big and *messy*. I thought *my* room was messy. Noah's would have won prizes. There was a big window, but the curtains were drawn and his ceiling light was on. The floor was covered with clothes, tapes and tape cases, open and closed books, empty pop cans. And in the middle of the mess was a battered Roland keyboard with a set of earphones plugged into the back. On two walls he had rock concert posters and on the other two walls, books. Hundreds of them. His bed was a four-poster with a big wooden cross hanging on a nail above it. Beside the cross was a picture of a woman and a little boy standing on a lawn in front of a house. It was Noah's house. Must be Noah and his mom, I thought.

"Want a drink?" asked Noah.

John and I said yes and Noah left the room.

My dad often told me that if you want to get to know somebody fast, you should look at his book-shelf. So that's what I did while Noah was out of the room. I stepped over some balled-up clothing and checked out a couple of the shelves. Wow. He had a lot of the usual stuff — a few Stephen Kings, some spy thrillers, Sherlock Holmes, and other cops-and-robbers stuff. A big hardcover copy of *The Exorcist*. But I also saw *Dracula*, *Frankenstein*, *A History of Witchcraft*, *Magic through the Ages*. And ghost books. *A Christmas Carol*, *Ghost Story*, *The Haunting of Hill House*, and one called *The Turn of the Screw*.

"Karen! He's coming back," John hissed.

I heard Noah's footsteps in the hall. I stepped away from the bookshelves, almost tripping on a pair of jeans as Noah came in with three glasses of juice on a tray.

"Here you go," he said, pushing some junk out of the way on his desk top and putting down the tray. "Why don't you sit down?"

John and I sat on the unmade bed and Noah sat on the chair at his desk. He said nothing. He took a sip of his orange juice and looked at me. He looked for so long I began to feel uncomfortable.

John spoke. "Ummm, your dad doesn't seem to like us being here. Maybe we should —"

"Don't pay any attention to him," Noah cut in. "I don't."

He looked my way again.

"Well, I guess you want to know why we're here," I said.

Noah nodded and swept his long hair back on his head. I could see his whole face now. Yup, I said to myself, he is cute.

Both Noah and John were staring at me, waiting for me to talk. So I started in. I told everything — about what we had seen on Chiefs' Island and about what had happened in our house. John fidgeted beside me as I spoke. When I had finished, Noah looked a little excited.

"Whose grave was it?" he asked.

"Ummm," John stuffed his hand into the pocket of his bathing suit as he spoke. "Cope something. Just a minute."

He pulled his hand out of his pocket again and unfolded a piece of paper.

"Yeah, Randall Copegog."

"He was the chief of the Ojibway band that lives on the Reserve. Copegog means 'fox' in English. That's what the newspaper said."

Fox. I thought about the stuff in the leather bag
— teeth, bones, a dried-up ear.

"He died a few days ago," Noah went on, "But
that probably wasn't his ghost you saw."

"How do you know that?" I asked.

Noah answered in his deep serious voice. "Well,
the guy you saw was dressed in traditional clothes,
right?" Without waiting for an answer he went on.
"And he had a medicine bag. Modern chiefs, as
far as I know, don't go in for that too much any
—"

"A *what*?"

"A medicine bag. That's what you found and
took home — probably."

"Oh, yeah, why didn't I think of that?" John
cut in. "I read something about them."

Noah nodded and took a long swallow of juice.

"Well," I said impatiently, "maybe you guys
know what a medicine bag is but I don't. Why
would anyone carry pills around in a *bag*?"

John started in with his Lecturing Voice. "Medicine doesn't mean like drugs. It means spiritual
power. In the old days at a certain age an Indian
male had to go out into the bush alone and go
without food and stuff like that. He hoped he'd
have a vision and find out what his totem animal
was. When he found out, he'd save sacred objects
connected with his totem and with his experiences.
Right, Noah?"

Noah nodded and his hair fell over his face.
"That's about it. Except that the medicine bag was
very powerful."

I thought about the little leather bag in my room

and the bones and dried-up ear and the coin. They didn't seem so powerful to me. I said so.

"*What*?" Noah almost jumped off his chair. "You *opened* it?"

"Yeah," I said. Then I added, "We wanted to see what was inside it." And felt stupid as soon as I said it.

Noah swept his hair back with a quick motion. The cross hanging from his ear swung back and forth. He began to talk fast.

"That's it! See, I couldn't figure out what the ghost on the island had to do with what seems to be going on in your house. So, think before you answer this. Were there any other times when funny stuff like last night happened in your house?"

John looked at me. I shook my head.

"Okay," Noah continued. "Don't you see the coincidence?"

"No," John said before I could.

"You opened the bag, right? You left the stuff you found in the bag in Karen's room, right? The poltergeist was playing outside Karen's room, right? What do you need, a ten-foot-high electric sign?"

"Polter*what*?" I said. I felt like things were getting out of control.

"Poltergeist. It's German. It means playful spirit."

"Yeah, well, I didn't think it was so playful. It scared the life out of me."

"Poltergeists *are* scary," Noah said calmly. "But they're not harmful. Usually. Anyway, like I was saying. Here's my theory. Opening the medicine bag released . . . um, let's call it a Power . . . in your house. It set something off, something spiritual, that was in your house all along. See? It's like, um . . . you tossed a pebble into a calm clear pool and the pebble set up ripples that spread across the surface.''

I understood what he was saying. And I didn't like it one bit. But I had a thought.

"So if I put the stuff back into the bag, and maybe get rid of the bag, things will be back to normal?''

"Well, maybe. But it's not that simple. When the spiritual activity starts it usually goes its own way. You know that old expression, Once the toothpaste is out of the tube it's hard to get it back in again.''

"You mean it's impossible.''

"Well, maybe. It's hard to say. But I think so.''

"So what else can we do?''

"Did you ever see *The Changeling*?''

"Is that the one where the composer rents an old house where a long time before a father murdered his son to get his inheritance?''

Noah looked happy and surprised that I knew the movie.

"Yeah, that's it! Well, remember the composer had to do a lot of research to find out about the house and who had lived there and stuff? I think you should find out as much as you can about your house. Is it new?''

"No,'' John seemed to come awake. Probably because Noah used the word "research.'' "It's over a hundred years old.''

"Well, maybe something happened there a long time ago. An accident. Maybe even a murder. You need to find out if you want to understand what's going on now.''

"Oh, great,'' I moaned. "That's all I need.''

Noah just sat there, looking at us.

"Well," John said. "I might be able to do the research. Not because I go for all this ghost stuff, understand. Just for the fun of it. Mom and Dad might be interested in finding out stuff about the history of our house. Mom would get off on that."

"And there's one more thing we could do," said Noah.

"Oh, what?"

"We could go over to Chiefs' Island tonight and try to talk to that ghost. And you could get rid of the medicine bag. Give it back to it — him."

Things really *were* getting out of hand. "No chance," I said. "It's spooky over there."

Noah talked calmly. While he explained why we had to go over to Chiefs' Island again it suddenly struck me. Here we were, three normal kids — well . . . pretty normal, I thought as I looked at Noah's pierced ear and long black hair, and at my brother, looking like a wet noodle with a notebook in its hand — talking calmly about *ghosts*. And two of us *believed* it all.

When Noah finished talking he looked at John.

"Okay with me," my brother said. "I wanted to go back anyway. But," he held up a finger and wagged it the way a teacher does when she wants to tell you how much hassle you'll get if you don't do what she says, "I want to go on record right now. I'm not saying what's been going on *isn't* ghosts, but I'm not saying it *is* either. I still think it's preternatural."

"Fair enough," Noah said. Then he looked at me, sweeping his hair back for the millionth time. He didn't say anything. I felt my brother's elbow dig into my ribs.

"Oh, all right," I said.

"When?" said John.

"Why not tonight?" Noah said. "There'll still be a full moon."

Why did I always think of werewolves and mouldy dead bodies whenever somebody said the words "full moon"?

"Hey," John cut in on my thoughts, "why not fix it with your dad so you can stay at our place tonight? Then you don't need to worry about what time we get back."

"Okay," Noah said, "but I'll need a few hours to get some equipment together. We gotta do this right."

You'd have thought he was planning a picnic.

9

Late Sunday Evening

Noah came over that night a little while after dinner with a big canvas sailor's bag full of stuff.

"What's *that*?" I said, closing the kitchen door behind him.

"Oh, just some ghost-hunting stuff." He smiled.

He had his long hair combed straight back on his head and held there with a barrette. The cross was still dangling from his ear.

"Where can I put it?" he asked, pointing to the bag.

"Come on upstairs. Hurry, before Minnie comes into the kitchen on a search-and-destroy mission and finds you here."

"Who's Minnie, your dog?"

I explained on the way up the back stairs.

We went to John's room. John was getting his stuff ready too. It was arranged in a row on his desk.

John's room was always neat. The only thing on

his floor was his rug and his furniture. His dresser drawers were always shut, without clothes spilling out of them. His bed was always made. His desk top was always clear. And his tapes and CD's were in their cases, stored in a box in alphabetical order. He drove me nuts.

On his wall was a big poster showing the DNA spiral with lots of coloured balls and sticks, and photos of planets and rockets from *Omni* magazine.

"Hey, let's see what you've got," he said to Noah when we came into his room.

Noah put down the bag and pulled the draw-strings. When he did that a picture of the little leather medicine bag flashed across my mind. He reached inside and pulled out a Sony portable video camera with a battery pack. He laid it on the desk. Next, one of those little idiot-proof thirty-five-millimetre cameras, with a built-in flash. Then a portable tape recorder. Then, on top of all that electronic gear he laid the wooden cross that I had seen hanging over his bed.

Next to Noah's stuff, John's candy bars and flashlights and bug lotion looked pretty lame.

"All *right*," John said when he saw all the gear. "Ghost Hunters Incorporated!"

He pulled open his desk drawer and said, "Look what I've got to add."

"Hey, wait a minute," I cut in. "You can't use those."

"Why not? They were just sitting in the base-ment, gathering dust."

"Because you can't, that's why."

"Yeah, I know, because they were Kenny's. Well, I think they've gone to waste long enough."

I looked at the two walkie-talkies on the desk.

They were red and white plastic — toys, really, but pretty powerful.

"Well I'm not using them."

"No sweat. Noah and I will use them. Right, Noah?"

"Whatever." Noah turned to me. "How about a look at the medicine bag?"

We sneaked out of the house about twelve-thirty. While we were waiting to leave, Mom and Dad had called from Vancouver to tell us they had arrived safe and to give us their phone number at their hotel. After that we'd waited for Skinny Minnie to hit the sack. I had made two trips to the door of the guest room at the far end of the hall and heard nothing. Minnie was dead to the world.

John had on his burglar-black outfit, same as Friday night. Noah was dressed in black too — even down to his deck shoes. I had on a navy-blue track suit, one with a hood. I wanted that to keep the mosquitoes out of my hair.

We stashed the two bags — Noah's sailor's bag and John's pack sack — in the bow of the rowboat and climbed in. John rowed. Noah and I sat scrunched together on the back seat. The medicine bag was buttoned in my shirt pocket. It felt warm.

I wasn't so sure I wanted to give the bag up. It scared me a bit, sure, and I supposed Noah was right about the bag unleashing some kind of power in our house. But I still sort of wished I could have kept it. In the boathouse maybe, not in my room.

Once we had cleared the shore Noah whispered to me, "Nervous?"

I jumped and he laughed. "I guess that answers my question."

"I just don't like the idea of being ripped apart by a werewolf or something."

Noah said calmly, in his deep commonsense voice, "Werewolf? You don't believe in *them*, do you?"

I was shocked. This guy was supposed to be the big expert on all this.

"Don't you?"

"Naw, that's just old legends and myths. Like vampires and talking skeletons."

"I read that there really *was* a Count Dracula," John cut in, puffing as he rowed.

"There was, and he was a bloodthirsty, nasty guy, but that's a long way from an undead dude with red eyes who creeps around at night in a cape sucking blood out of people's necks."

"And turns himself into a bat or a wolf," John added.

I was getting mixed up. "Wait a minute. What are you doing here, then?"

"Because I think ghosts are real, that's why. Or could be. I also think we shouldn't be afraid of them. They won't hurt us. At least that's my opinion."

"Sorry, but that doesn't make me feel any better."

"Yeah, well, I don't blame you. I mean, there's an awful lot of nonsense floating around about the occult and the supernatural and all that. And the biggest lie of all, as far as I'm concerned, is the idea that ghosts come back to hurt people. I know some people believe that, but I don't.

"All the movies and books nowadays are based on that," John said.

"Right. That's what I call the Revenge Theory.

Like in *The Changeling*. Remember, Karen? The ghost of the little boy wants revenge on the rich famous Senator. Who ends up dead. Most movies and books are based on the Revenge Theory.''

"Sure, because that makes a more interesting story," John said, resting on the oars for a moment. "Blood and guts and stuff.''

"Right," Noah answered.

I didn't feel any less scared, but I was sort of half interested.

"What other theories do you have?''

"Well, there's the English Castle Theory. In England they've got tons of old castles and manors and houses and bridges and a lot of them supposedly have a ghost haunting them. The ghost is there because of something — usually some kind of disaster, like a murder or horrible accident or wrecked love affair — and it just sort of hangs around. It *appears*. It doesn't try to make contact with live people and it doesn't try to hurt anyone.''

"So that's the theory you like," I said.

"Nope, I think it's dumb too — probably. I think those ghosts are dreamed up by tourist bureaus.''

I was beginning to wonder if Weird Noah ever gave a straight answer.

"Why do you think it's wrong?" John puffed. He was pulling at the oars again.

While Noah talked, I tuned out and looked down the lake toward the narrows. It was a beautiful night, calm, with no wind, and a big silver moon splashing light on the water. The oars creaked as John rowed, and the bow whispered to the water. I could have stayed out there all night. Except that me and two crazy boys were going to find a *ghost*.

I tuned back in to what Noah was saying.

"Do you remember Marley's ghost?"

"Yeah," I said, "from *A Christmas Carol*. What about him?"

"Hey!" John put in. "Maybe Karen and I didn't see *anyone* Friday night. Maybe it was an undigested bit of beef! Or a fragment of an underdone potato!"

Noah laughed and said to me, "Marley warned Scrooge that if he didn't change his skinflint ways he would end up like Marley, right?"

"Right."

"So Marley was condemned to walk the earth and see humans suffering and not be able to help them. He had the chance to help people when he was alive, but he didn't. All he cared about then was money. Now he wants to help, but he can't. So he suffers, too. See? It's kind of, like, *moral* suffering. Marley warns Scrooge to change his ways so he can avoid that."

I tried one more time. "Is this the theory you follow?"

"Mostly."

I groaned.

"My idea is that a ghost is a dead person —"

"Brilliant!" I cut in. "Wonderful —"

"— who can't get into heaven or wherever we go when we die because he has to atone for something first."

"A-tone?"

"Yeah. It means, like —"

Before Noah could answer, the boat ground up onto the rock on the shore of the island.

"We're here," John announced. As if we didn't know.

A few minutes later we were ready. We wrestled the rowboat well up onto the rock shelf, with the oars and life jackets stowed inside. We had bug lotion smeared on our hands, necks and faces. I pulled my hood up and tied the drawstrings.

John and Noah had the walkie-talkies hung on their belts, like cops on TV. Noah looked like a newsman with his video camera and battery pack and a tape recorder hung around his neck.

I got to carry the cross. I wondered why a guy who didn't believe in werewolves and vampires brought a cross with him, but I didn't say anything.

John led the way, peering at his compass and then heading into the trees. We walked slowly in the dark bush, twisting and ducking and stepping over fallen logs. After a long while John's breathless voice hissed that the clearing was just ahead. We crept to the edge of the trees. All the night noises had faded away.

"Hang on," Noah whispered, "I wanna get a shot of the whole place."

He knelt and brought the camera up to his eye and panned slowly across the graveyard. The place looked the same as it had two nights before — the moonlight making the leaning gravestones glow and throwing gloomy twisted shadows across the clearing.

"Okay, done."

Noah lowered the camera. He switched on the tape recorder and whispered, "Where do we find your ghost?"

"This way," John said.

He began to move to the left through the trees, counting his steps. He stopped and dropped to his knees. Without thinking, I did too. The three of us crawled slowly to the edge of the trees. Then we peered into the clearing.

At the far end of the graveyard, sitting on the same new headstone, was the Indian, staring into the trees to our left. He was dressed the same way, he was sitting the same way, ankles crossed, hands on his knees, looking relaxed — and he was just as terrifying. That strange light showed every detail of his clothing and his face. Luckily, we couldn't see his eyes at that angle.

Out of the corner of my eye I saw Noah bring the camera up again. "This is *great*!" he whispered as he began to shoot. When he brought the camera down again John talked, his voice trembling.

"Maybe . . . maybe we should just take his picture and get out of here."

"Yeah," I whispered, holding the cross in front of me.

"No way I'm leaving without checking that guy out!" Noah said in hushed tones. "Besides, we agreed you're going to give back the bag."

"Well," I said, "we could just leave it here."

"Or toss it to him and run," John whispered.

Instead of saying anything more, Noah got to his feet and stepped into the clearing. He stopped dead.

"Wow!" he said out loud. "It's *freezing*!"

John stood and followed. I didn't intend to wait for them alone, so I went too.

Noah led us slowly, step by step, toward the Indian on the gravestone. Our feet swished through the damp grass. The Indian seemed to be sleeping or dreaming. He didn't move a muscle.

We kept walking over the cold uneven ground, side by side now. Noah held the camera at chest level and I could see his hand squeezing the trigger. He was shooting. I held the cross in front of me, feeling silly. And scared.

When we were about twenty feet from the old man his head slowly turned and he faced us.

Close up, his craggy mask-like face was almost inhuman. His long hair was pulled back from his wrinkled face and held tight by the leather headband. He had thick eyebrows and broad cheeks. His mouth was a hard straight line under his large flat nose.

It was his eyes that got to me, though. Deep black wells with tiny red fires at the bottoms under the heavy brows. Eyes that seemed to nail me down, or stab through me. When he looked at me I felt trapped.

We stopped. Nobody said anything.

My heart was pounding. My breath clouds were coming faster and faster. So were John's and Noah's. But the Indian had none.

"The bag," Noah hissed. "Give him the bag."

I switched the cross to my left hand. My right hand slowly unzipped my track top and unbuttoned my shirt pocket. I drew out the bag and held it out in front of me.

Nothing. The red light glowed on the Sony — Noah was still shooting. I could hear the tape revolving in the recorder.

I couldn't take the tension anymore so I quickly walked forward and shook the bag. I heard feet swishing in the grass behind me.

"Ummm, John and I found this the other night. We think it's yours," I said in a cracked voice. I waited, half expecting a blood-freezing shriek or a wolf howl.

But a big grin split the Indian's face, lighting up his eyes.

"Yep, that bag, she's mine all right."

His voice was rough, like pebbles scraping around in a pail. And it seemed to come from miles away.

He held out his hand and I dropped the bag onto his wrinkled palm. He slipped one of the bag's drawstrings up under his belt and tied the bag on. His belt was decorated with quills and coloured beads, just like the bag.

His grin disappeared and his face was like a carved wooden mask again.

Silence.

I stood there shaking, holding the cross out, keeping it between me and the spooky figure on the gravestone, wondering if it would do any good.

John's voice sounded strained. "Uh, do you live around here?"

Boy, could he come up with stupid questions sometimes!

"Yep." The Indian's body seemed to relax a bit. He pulled at his earlobe. He had big ears.

More silence. It's hard to think of something to say when you're in a forbidden graveyard at midnight and you're standing across from an old, half-naked man you think might be a ghost.

The Indian didn't look cold, but I was freezing. John and Noah were shivering like they'd been tobogganing in their underwear for the last two hours. And the Indian had that sort of glow that he'd had two nights ago. I could tell now that it wasn't from the moonlight.

"Would you mind telling us your name?" Noah asked politely.

"Nope. I'm Chief Copegog. How 'bout you?"

I looked at the gravestone. Behind the Indian's leather leggings I could make out part of the name Copegog carved into the marble. Was he the ghost of the guy buried there?

"I'm Noah, this is John and this is Karen. We live across the lake there, in town."

"Uh, huh. Haven't bin that place in a long time." Noah kept going. "Do you live on the Reserve?"

"Nope. Right here."

Boy, I thought, talking to this guy is like pulling teeth.

Noah pointed to the medicine bag hanging from the Indian's belt. "Nice bag."

The Indian slid from the gravestone and the three of us jumped back. I held out the cross with both hands, stiffly, the way the cops on TV hold their guns. I was surprised at how short the Indian was — a little smaller than John. But he had a wide chest and powerful shoulders and arms, like my dad. He turned to go.

"No, Chief Copegog, don't go!" John shouted. The Indian turned back.

"Ummmm," John was frantically trying to think of something to say. "Can we come and visit you again?"

"Free country, I guess."

"Um, would you like us to bring you anything?"

The Indian creased his brow and thought for a moment. "Got any tobacco? Sure could use a smoke."

"Uh, sure, we could get some," John answered.

"Chief Copegog, how long is it since you had a smoke?" Noah asked.

Another stupid question, I thought. Then I realized what Noah was getting at.

The Indian pulled at his ear some more. No wonder his ears were big.

"Must be . . . what's the year now?"

Noah told him.

"Yep. Hundred fifty years or so since I had a smoke."

"A hun —"

Noah cut John off. "What kinda tobacco would you like?"

"Regular kind, she's okay."

He turned to go again. Then he slowly turned back.

And looked right into my eyes, as if he could see into my mind. His eyes were like two red flashlight beams in there, looking around at my thoughts.

"Might be you got too many troubles for one girl."

I could feel my jaw drop as he began to walk away, rolling his body from side to side, like a sailor. He was pigeon-toed. But he sort of *floated* over the ground. When he got to the trees he disappeared like a faint light blinking off.

I stared after him, lost in my thoughts. What did he mean by what he said to me? How did *he* know about my "troubles"?

John's voice yanked me back. "Noah, can I have the camera? I want to get pictures of the gravestones."

Noah turned his back to John so John could fish out the little camera. Soon the clearing was being zapped with quick flashes of white light, as if a firefly were saying hello to all the headstones.

"Hey, Karen, look."

Noah was crouched down looking at the bare earth in front of the grave. He shone a flashlight, playing the round patch of light back and forth across the ground.

There were no footprints.

Noah turned to me, his face bright with excitement.

"What we got here is a genuine, authentic, walking, talking ghost."

He stood up. "And," he smiled, patting the Sony, "we got him on tape!"

day four

10

Monday Morning

We didn't get back to the boathouse until two-thirty in the morning. Noah was babbling on about talking to the ghost again, and getting it all on videotape. John was babbling too, saying "preternatural" as often as he could, but I could tell he was hooked on the *super*natural.

Me? I was in bad shape, but I tried not to let it show. Besides being scared to death by that Indian and his faraway gravelly voice and the fact that he could just *disappear* like that, I was really rattled when he talked to me. What did he mean?

So I kept pretty quiet all the way back to our house. And I didn't say a word when John and Noah made noises about putting the tape Noah shot on the VCR right away.

The three of us went into the living room. While Noah took the tape out of the camera, fit it into an adapter and put it in the VCR, John slipped up the stairs to make sure Skinny Minnie was still sleeping.

"No sweat," he announced when he returned. "She's still in munchkin land."

Noah had the VCR ready to go. He pushed the button on the remote. We sat in a row on the couch, on the edge, like winkies watching *The Twilight Zone*.

We saw a lot of shadows, for a long time. We saw some gravestones. The picture jumped and jittered when we got to the part where Noah had walked toward Chief Copegog. We even saw the new gravestone that marked the new grave.

But no ghost.

Noah swore. "Nothing. He didn't show up on the tape!"

"Let's look again," John suggested.

While they played with the machinery, I went into the kitchen and poured myself a tall glass of cold milk. I sat down at the kitchen table. The only light was the one over the stove that we had left on when we sneaked out of the house. My hand shook as I lifted the glass to my mouth.

I turned to look out the window. I froze. Kenny was outside, staring at me through the glass! I cried out and my glass crashed to the floor.

"You idiot!" I said to myself, after I realized that I was looking at my own reflection in the window.

My hands shook as I soaked up the spilled milk from the floor with a dishrag and swept up the bits of glass.

I knew I wasn't going to get to sleep too soon, so I kicked off my Nikes and padded into my dad's study to dig up a book to read. As soon as I switched on the big lamp over his drafting table I saw that something was wrong.

His charcoal sticks were lying all over the table top. One sheet of paper was in the middle of the table, smudged and smeared, but in the centre of the paper was this:

What the heck was going on? I turned the paper around, looking at the marks from different angles. What was it? And who did it? None of *us* could have done this. And I knew my dad would never leave his desk like that. In fact, if he saw the messy paper and his sticks broken and scattered, he'd have a fit. He was a real nut about what he liked to call "a clean workplace." Would Minnie have been fooling around with Dad's stuff? I doubted it.

I tidied everything up, trying to put the strange marks on the paper out of my mind. I put the charcoal back, balled up the paper and threw it into the big wicker wastebasket. After taking a last look around, I grabbed a book of Herman cartoons and turned out the light.

When I got to the kitchen again I found John and Noah tying up their packs.

"What's up?"

"The audio-tape didn't turn up anything either, John answered, "so Noah thinks we might as well go back to Chiefs' Island again tonight. We're going over to Miracle Mart to get some tobacco. It's open all night."

I told them I thought they were crazy. And when they asked me to come with them I told them I *knew* they were crazy.

"Come on, Karen. Maybe he'll talk to you again. He seems to be interested in you," Noah said.

"No way. Not ever. Besides," I added, "won't your father wonder where you are?"

"I told him I was staying here overnight, remember? Besides," Noah said bitterly, "he doesn't care *where* I am — and vice versa."

After they left I climbed up the back stairs, went into my room, slid the bolt home, and clicked on my desklamp. Boy, was I tired. I could feel a prize winner of a headache coming on. I dragged off my clothes and put on Dad's old blue Western University Wrestling Team T-shirt. It fit like a tent and was great for sleeping in, especially in hot weather.

I pulled the chain on my bed lamp, splashing a little pool of yellow light on my unmade bed. Then I went to the window and pulled the curtains closed. The last thing I wanted to see when I got up was Chiefs' Island floating out there on the lake. I stepped over to my desk and just before I clicked off the light I noticed that something was wrong.

Ever since I saw that old movie, *Razor Blade*,

where a crazy guy who had escaped from a nut-house hid in a big walk-in closet in someone's house and slit the throats of the whole family one by one — ever since then I've *always* kept my closet door closed. And locked, with one of those hook-and-eye latches.

Now the little hook hung uselessly and the door stood open about six inches.

I groaned. I was *sick* of mysteries. Sick and scared.

Then I thought maybe Mom or Dad had been in there for some reason before they left. But why? They never came into my room without asking me. I dashed over to the door and slammed it shut and slid the hook into the eye bolt.

I climbed wearily into my waterbed and started leafing through the *Herman* book. I couldn't stop myself from smiling. John and I always argued about the proper way to read a *Herman* book. I liked to open it anywhere and read, then flip and read, backward and forward. That drove John nuts. He'd start at page one and work through the book, cartoon by cartoon, like he was reading *Peter Pan*. He laughed at the nutty cartoons as much as I did, though.

I flipped and read, trying to find something funny, trying to get tired. But I didn't. The stuff that had happened lately — the ghost of the Indian and the scary events in the house — played in my head like scratchy background music. I tried to block the thoughts out, but I couldn't.

I dropped the book onto the blanket. What was happening? I thought, and began to cry. Why is it happening to me? John and Noah were having fun, but I wasn't. I didn't know why, but I started to think about Kenny and the ache inside me flared up like a wound. Why couldn't things be like they used to be? I said out loud, crying harder.

As if they were answering me, the wind chimes tinkled.

I looked up. The chimes, blurred by my tears, hung motionless. But the tinkling turned to jangling.

And the louder and more violently the chimes jangled, the colder the room got.

I squeezed my eyes shut and clapped my hands over my ears. "No, no, no," I begged. "No more!"

The chimes stopped jangling. Outside my room in the hall I heard a quick skittering laugh, then footsteps running away. I lay back and pulled the blankets over my head.

Silence. I peeked out, staring at my door, waiting. Sure enough, footsteps crept down the hall toward my room, creaking on the hardwood floor.

Bang! Bang! Bang! on the door. The banging went on and on, getting louder and louder, filling the cold air with the terrifying racket. The door shook in its frame. *Bang! Bang! Bang! Bang! Bang!*

Then the doorknob began to rattle and shake as if a huge hand, frustrated, was trying to rip it out of the wood.

I cowered in my bed, moaning and shivering. I was paralyzed, unable to do anything. I thought the pounding and rattling was going to drive me crazy.

Finally the deafening noise faded and the footsteps walked away down the hall toward the front of the house. I thought I heard them on the front stairs, but the stairs were carpeted so I couldn't be sure.

I began to calm down. And the calmer I got, the madder I got. I'd had enough!

I climbed out of my waterbed and sat on the edge. I was shivering and my toes felt the way they did when I'd been skating on the lake too long — icy and stiff. My fingers were stiff, too.

I heaved myself to my feet and stepped across the frigid rug to the door. I put my hand on the knob. Icy.

Footsteps ran down the hall toward me!

I dropped my hand and practically flew across the room, and jumped into the bed. The water rolled back and forth, lifting and dropping me.

Laughter outside my room, echoing in the hall.

Then I heard strange noises on the floor out there. Something hard being dragged across the wood. And *click, click, click,* like two pieces of plastic tapping together. The noises would go to the end of the hall, then come back.

And the full force of the cold came with them.

I lay down, trying to keep control. I was trapped — too scared to open my door, feeling like my mind was being stretched too thin and that it was going to break soon. I had a monster headache that banged away inside my skull.

After I don't know how long the clicking and the footsteps stopped moving back and forth. I drifted off to sleep — at least I think it was sleep. Every once in a while I'd hear the wind chimes and I'd scrunch down under the covers, pinched by the cold.

And once I heard *thump, thump, thump,* outside the door.

I remember waking one time and looking at my

clock radio. Five-fifteen. It was quiet in the house so I hopped out of bed, ran to the window, and drew the curtains. I scooted back into bed. I knew it would be dawn soon and I knew that I wouldn't sleep right until I saw the light.

A little later I heard noises in the kitchen. Noah and John were back. That's when I fell asleep.

I came down to breakfast late, about ten-thirty, wearing yellow terry shorts and a white T-shirt. I couldn't sleep anymore. My headache wouldn't let me. Noah and John were sitting at the table. Noah was wearing black jeans and a white T-shirt with black letters that said ACID RAIN KILLS. He was chasing a few soggy Cheerios around with a spoon in half a bowl of milk and John was shovelling some kind of mess into his mouth — I could see cottage cheese and strawberries but I couldn't recognize what else was in there. And I didn't want to know. He had on Reebok jogging shorts — although he never jogged anywhere in his *life* — and an O.D. tank top.

There was still some tea in the pot so I poured a cup and sat down, holding my head.

"He wasn't there," Noah said.

"Huh? Who wasn't where?"

"Chief Copegog. When we went back with the cigars, he wasn't there. And the graveyard was, like, normal temperature. So we put the cigars and a book of matches on the gravestone and left."

"*Cigars*? You bought him *cigars*?"

"Yeah," said John past the goop in his mouth. "White Owls. Big ones."

Noah looked embarrassed. "It was all we could think of."

I didn't care anyway. I didn't want to know.

"We're gonna go over to the library and get into some heavy research on this house," John continued. "Spend the whole day there. Noah figures there must have been some kind of disaster happened here. That's what's causing the poltergeist to appear."

"Too bad we only have one occurrence," Noah said, sweeping his hair back from his face, sounding really professional. I could tell that was the kind of word he read in his ghost-hunting books — "occurrence."

"Two," I said before I thought about it. After I said it I wished I had kept my mouth shut.

"You mean —" John's jaw dropped, revealing a white and red pudding inside his mouth.

"Yeah."

I told them all about it. Noah took notes, like a newspaper reporter, and asked me questions.

"So the only thing different last night were the two strange noises?"

"Yeah."

"And you can't place them, eh? You don't have any idea what they were?"

"Nope. A click and drag, a thumping sound."

"Were you scared?" John put in.

I shot him a Boy Are You Dumb look and took a sip of tea.

Then, "Hey, wait. No, it's probably nothing," I said.

"What?" said Noah. "*What?*"

He slapped his notebook on the table.

"Just a second."

I hauled myself from my chair and walked down the hall to the study. When I came back I tossed a ball of drafting paper to Noah.

Noah unscrunched the white paper and flattened it out on the kitchen table, smudging the charcoal lines a little.

We looked at it.

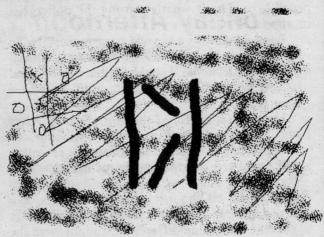

"Doesn't mean anything to me," John said. "Dad probably did it and forgot to clean up."

"As if he would," I shot back.

Noah scrunched up the paper again. "Let's go to the library," he said to John. "That doesn't mean anything." As the two boys stood up to go he added, "I don't think."

After John and Noah left for the library I cleaned up the kitchen and climbed the stairs to my room.

I locked the door once I was inside. Warm morning sunlight poured through the window, spilling gold across the floor. I unhooked the lock on my closet, drew a breath, and pulled the door open fast.

Nothing. I locked it again.

I fell onto the waterbed, pulling the covers over me, and fell asleep.

Monday Afternoon

Someone was pounding at my bedroom door! The doorknob rattled and the door rumbled in its frame.

I rolled over and faced the wall, pulling the blankets over my head.

I won't listen to that anymore! I won't! I thought.

The pounding kept up.

"Karen, wake up!" It was John's voice.

I stuck my head out from under the covers.

Blinding sunlight shot through the window, stabbing into my eyes. I rolled over again and faced the door. I felt hot and my mouth was sticky. I still had my clothes on.

I dragged my body out of bed and unlocked the door. "Come on in," I croaked.

John and Noah tumbled into the room like two kindergarten kids, practically knocking me down.

Noah's eyes flashed. "I was right! I think." For once he didn't sound like a forty-year-old.

"Sure you were right. We found it. For sure."
John was breathless. He was chewing bubble gum
and after he said that he pumped out a huge bubble, big as his face. I could never understand why
the gum didn't stick to his braces. Above the big
pink bubble his blue eyes sparkled. He sucked the
air back into his mouth so the bubble collapsed
slowly and drooped on his chin.

"What's the big deal?" I asked, not sure I wanted
to know. Then I said, "What time is it?"

John ignored me and started to talk. "We spent
half the day in the —"

"About three o'clock," Noah cut in.

"— library reading until our eyeballs were ready
to fall —"

"— I never read so much at one time in my life!
This brother of yours is a —"

"— out and our nostrils were full of dust from
old books and —"

"— microfilm! Wow, that stuff is like reading
fuzzy words through binoculars! Talk about —"

"*Stop!*"

I had my hands clapped over my ears and my eyes
shut. I was sitting on the bed. John and Noah were
still standing at the open door. John's hand gripped
the knob as if he wanted to tear it off. Both of them
looked like puppies who just stumbled on a spilled
bag of Milkbone. Their mouths hung open. I
guessed I had shocked them.

"Sorry," John said in a low voice. "Do you have
one of your headaches?"

"Yeah."

"Why don't you take a pill?" Noah suggested,
almost whispering.

"It won't help her," John answered for me, a little of his Lecturing tone creeping in. "She gets these migraines. Pills don't help. Nothing helps. She started getting them after our brother —"

I shot him a look and he shut up. Noah looked embarrassed.

"Anyway," he said, "want to hear what we found out, Karen?"

I was still boiling hot from my sleep under the covers. My head felt like it was full of taffy.

"Let's take a swim first," I said.

The three of us were lying side by side on the dock. The late-afternoon sun was sinking behind the house and our shore of the lake was shaded and cool. But Chiefs' Island was still brightly lit and over the calm water I could see the flat rock where we had landed on our trips to the graveyard. There was a light breeze whispering in the weeping willow.

"Well," Noah was saying, "we made progress at the library."

"Yeah, after we got that old twig of a librarian to let us into the so-called historical archives we started checking local histories."

"And they led us to the microfilms of old newspapers."

"How about skipping all the dramatics and getting to the point," I said. I guess I sounded mean, cutting into their big moment, but I didn't really feel like waiting till doomsday.

"Okay, okay," John said, sounding a little hurt. "Here's the straight stuff."

He cleared his throat as he sat up and wrapped his arms around his knees and started in with his Lecturing Voice.

"Our house was built around a century and a half ago by a rich bachelor named Bond who got his money from the lumber and sawmill business, lawyering, and some inheritance."

"Not what you'd call poor," Noah added. He had sat up, too. His wet hair was slicked straight back and the two studs and cross in his ear winked in the light.

"No, and from what we could gather, he wasn't Mister Nice Guy either. He turned up in the newspapers once in a while."

"Like when he built his house — your house — on the shore of the lake on property he cheated away from an old lady whose financial affairs he was handling."

"Right," John said. "Anyway, he was loaded, and he had three servants who lived in the attic. An old manservant named Oliver, a cook named McCullough, and her eighteen-year-old daughter, who did the housecleaning."

"You forgot the drinking," Noah said.

"Huh? Oh, yeah. Bond was a drinker. Famous for it. A real prize winner. Anyway, he got in trouble for beating up the manservant one time. Broke the poor old guy's nose. According to the paper, the old guy refused to press charges, plus he kept working for Bond.

"But the juicy gossip was that he got engaged to the young woman. We read the wedding announcement in the paper."

"Sounds romantic, right?" Noah held up his hand and moved it across in front of his face, writing on the air with his finger. "Rich snobby lawyer marries servant. Nice headline."

"Except he didn't," John cut in.

"Nope. But he *did* get her pregnant, from what we can figure. The paper just hinted about that. Anyway, she hanged herself."

I sat up quickly. "In *our* house?" A pain shot through my head.

"No, no, her mother and her quit and moved out. She hanged herself in a boardinghouse."

"The mother left town soon after," John continued.

I wondered when they were going to get to the point. All that stuff sounded like a soap opera. I mean, I knew it was a terrible tragedy for the woman and her mother and I was sure the rich lawyer-drunk was a creep, but it had happened about a hundred and fifty years ago and right then I had other things on my mind.

"Then," Noah said, "the lawyer beat up the manservant again. Real bad. But he still didn't press charges."

"Oh?" I said when Noah paused. I knew I was supposed to say something. "Why not?"

"Because," John announced, "a few days later, the lawyer was found dead."

"By a neighbour," Noah said. "In your house."

"In the hall outside your bedroom," John added. "In a big pool of blood."

"With a long knife in his chest."

"He had been dead for days," John added, "so he —"

"Yeah, yeah, I get the point," I cut in.

I twisted my body and looked at our house. The back wall was shadowed and the windows reflected the sky so I couldn't see in. The windows looked like cold blank eyes. Behind me I heard the wind sighing in the willow and the wavelets lapping the shore and the crib of the dock.

It wasn't exactly good news to find out that somebody had murdered a nasty rich creep in the house I lived in. I imagined the dead lawyer dressed in one of those long black coats with a high white stiff collar and a diamond pin in his tie, lying in the hall upstairs with a knife handle sticking out of his chest, thick red blood leaking onto the hardwood, staining it. I suddenly felt chilly.

I looked at John. He was hooked. The sparkle in his blue eyes told me that. And Noah kept sweeping his wet hair back, trying to look calm.

"So what do we do now?" I asked. "How can we keep living in a house where a dead guy is marching up and down the hall all night and making strange noises and pounding on doors? Should we phone Vancouver and tell Mom and Dad and ask them to come home? They won't believe us, will they?"

"Nope," John answered. "Remember a couple of years ago when you went kind of nutty and —"

"Yeah, I remember."

"There's one thing you guys haven't thought about," Noah cut in.

I sat up and pulled my knees to my chest to keep warm. I turned to face the weeping willow. The long branches trailed in the water and the long thin leaves moved gently in the breeze. I didn't want to look at our house anymore. And no way did I want to look out over the lake.

"What's that?" John asked.

"Well, we've been assuming the ghost is the lawyer. It could be the young woman he got in trouble, the one who hanged herself. Or it's even possible it's the old manservant."

I barely listened to Noah. I was staring at the willow, remembering the times Kenny and I played in it, climbing up, scraping our hands and arms on the rough bark. We built a tree house there once. And whenever one of us felt bad or got into trouble, we'd go there and the other one would know where to look.

"Yeah, right!" John exclaimed. "It could be. Or maybe all three of them! Maybe — Karen! What's the matter?"

I was crying. I tried to stop it, tried to dam up the tears, but I couldn't. They flowed harder and harder and I began to sob. I felt my face get hot and twisted. The willow tree blurred and sank away.

"Why can't it be the way it used to be?" I sobbed. "Why did everything have to change?"

Then I lost control and cried and spluttered and sniffed. I tried to hide my hot face with my hands.

I stood up. My brother and Noah watched me silently. It was one of those times nobody could say anything and they knew that.

I walked to where the dock met the grassy shore, then stepped into the water. I waded crying into the lake.

12

Late Monday Afternoon

Our family didn't go to church. Both my parents were good people, with very strong morals. I mean, they knew what was right and wrong and when John or I even *looked* like we might do something wrong, they got on our case fast. And they were kind — always doing things for our neighbours or other members of the family. They even had a foster kid in the Dominican Republic or somewhere. But church was no part of my growing up. My dad told me one time a church was just like a club and he didn't want to be a member.

I was thinking about that as I walked up Neywash Street. I was thinking, maybe if we *did* belong to a religion like a lot of kids in my class, maybe I wouldn't be so mixed up. Maybe all this horrible stuff wouldn't be happening to me.

It was about five o'clock and the bells in the tower of the big Presbyterian church were playing some kind of hymn. The loud heavy notes rolled out of the tower like waves.

I wasn't sure when I had decided to try to talk with Noah's father. I guess it was when I was standing up to my neck in the lake with Noah and John watching me like hawks from the dock and I realized no matter where I looked I couldn't escape the bad feelings that seemed to own my mind. If I looked toward our house I thought of a horrible puffed-up corpse in the hall outside my room. If I looked out over the lake I saw Chiefs' Island and thought about the ghost of Chief Copegog stuck in that depressing graveyard when he could have been . . . wherever ghosts are *supposed* to be. He didn't look too happy the two times I saw him. I felt sorry for him now — when I wasn't scared to death by him. And if Noah was right, it had been his medicine bag that had started all that poltergeist stuff.

When I looked toward the willow tree or the boathouse, all I could think about was Kenny and the good times we used to have, playing there. The big hole inside me that had been there since Kenny went away, the big empty space filled with pain — that was worse than the scary stuff. And I didn't know how to get rid of the hurt. I felt trapped.

So I was walking up Neywash, going to see a minister. Maybe he could help. Maybe Mom and Dad wouldn't like it, but I didn't know what else to do. Besides, they were in Vancouver.

I rang the doorbell of the big brick house. No answer. I rang it again. Nothing.

Then I heard music. There was a flagstone walk that went around the side of the house. I followed it and found myself in a big back yard. It was mostly grass but there was a huge flower garden with a riot of colours and odours from dozens of kinds of flowers I didn't know the names of. The drone of slow dull hymns came from a portable radio on top of a picnic table.

In the middle of the garden, on his hands and knees, was Noah's father.

He was wearing a black short-sleeved shirt with the collar open and long tan-coloured pants. He had on those black rubber boots with the red band around the top that your mother makes you wear on rainy days. He was scratching at the dirt around some yellow flowers with one of those claw tools. His hands were dirty. I waited and after a moment he looked up and saw me.

His forehead wrinkled and his thick dark eyebrows jumped toward each other.

"Good afternoon, dear." He raised himself to his knees. "You're Noah's friend, aren't you?"

"Yes, sir, sort of. We just met."

"Ah."

I looked at the toes of my shoes, thinking, maybe this hadn't been such a good idea after all. He waited.

"Um, could I talk to you for a second, sir? If you're not too busy," I added.

"Not at all, dear, not at all." He smiled again. "If you don't mind my working while we talk. That'll be all right, won't it? I don't get much chance to keep the weeds at bay."

"Sure, sure. That's fine."

He dropped to all fours and started scratching again.

The sinking sun shone on his bald head. The head was beaded with sweat and it bobbed up and down as he worked.

"How can I help you, dear?" he said to the ground.

It was hard to talk to the top of his head. "Um, I wanted to ask you, sir —"

"People call me Reverend Webster, dear, not Sir."

"Oh, sorry, sir — I mean Reverend Webster."

He kept digging and scratching, moving slowly from one bunch of flowers to another. He moved to some white ones with lots of blooms on them.

"Um," I started again. "Do you . . . are there . . ."

He raised himself to his knees again. "Yes, dear, go ahead."

"Ghosts?"

His brow wrinkled. "I beg your pardon. Ghosts? What do you mean?"

"Are there ghosts? Do they exist?"

His eyebrows jumped again. "Of course not."

He dropped down and scratched furiously. Maybe I got him mad, I thought.

He started talking to the freshly dug earth. "The Bible speaks of an afterlife, of course, and all God-fearing people believe in Heaven and Hell. When we die, our sins are weighed in the balance, and if we have lived by the precepts of Our Lord Jesus Christ, and if we have accepted Him as our Saviour, we will live for eternity in the presence of Almighty God."

He grunted and crushed a clod of black earth.

"If we follow the ways of the Devil, we will live

forever alienated from God's presence. That's what hell *is* — not being with God. But ghosts — that's just nonsense, dear.''

He looked up at me. There was a smudge of dirt on his forehead.

"And it's dangerously sacrilegious.''

I took a deep breath and said to the top of his head, ''Do we . . . in heaven, do we meet our family? See, I had this brother —''

"Yes, in a way. They are there, if they have lived as I just described. But our souls belong to God, not our family, and it is to Him that we give our attention.''

"But, I mean, will I ever *see* him again, that's what I want to know.''

He looked up. ''I'm sure you will, dear.'' But he didn't sound like he meant it.

I tried again. ''What if . . . what if you think you've seen a ghost? Aren't there lots of people who have?''

"Now you're sounding like Noah. Those stories are the record of poor, ignorant, misguided people. They're not true.''

"But, if there's an afterlife, how come there can't be ghosts? Isn't it possible —''

He rose to his knees again and pointed the claw tool at me.

"My dear girl, you must stop this. Ghosts are folklore. Entertaining, perhaps, at parties and in books. You must not confuse them with the living reality of the revealed word of God. What church do you attend?''

"Well, my family doesn't go to church.''

"Ah.'' He said that little word as if it explained everything. ''Perhaps if your parents brought you to our church . . . Yes, you ask them to do that, dear. This Sunday. Then we can talk further.''

He dropped down and started in on the plants. "Well, um, thanks, Reverend.''

"You're welcome, dear. Come back any time.''

On my way home I felt stupid and embarrassed and mad. I was mad at myself because I had probably sounded like a winkie, blabbering on about ghosts and heaven in one sentence and about Kenny in the next. My face burned, I felt so stupid.

Then I got really mad at *him* — Noah's father. What *good* was he, anyway? And how come it was okay to believe in a place where you sat around on a cloud all day and plucked a harp but it was wrong and *dangerous* to believe in Chief Copegog — who I had seen with my own eyes?

And that was when I decided who I had to talk to. The only one who could help. Who do you talk to if you want to know about ghosts?

A ghost, that's who.

13

Monday Evening

Minnie cooked us baked spaghetti for supper and left it in the oven. By the time we got to it the pasta was dry and hard and tasteless. On the table was a note telling us she had gone to Barrie with some friends and she'd be back later.

After supper John went to call on Noah. They were going to work in the library until it closed, to find out more about the murder in our house.

I went into John's room and got his pack. I knew it would be hanging on the back of his closet door like it always was. When I opened it I saw that he had all the stuff in there — flashlights, knife, bug lotion — ready for another trip to Chiefs' Island. I stuffed my wool sweater into it, strapped it up and headed for the boathouse. I had decided not to take any of Noah's stuff — the camera or tape recorder or the big wooden cross. I had no use for all that.

I had a couple of hours of light left, so I might

be able to get back before dark. I knew everybody would wonder where I had gone and that I'd get into a hassle when John and Noah found out I'd gone without them, but I didn't care too much about that.

I was lucky there was no wind. I made it across to the island pretty easily. I'm not too strong but I'm a pretty good rower. I had trouble hauling the boat up onto the shore, though, so I just tied it to a tree and let it float. I was in a hurry.

I stopped to rub on some bug dope and threw the pack onto my back and cut into the bush. I didn't know how to use a compass like John did, so I tried to walk in a straight line from the shore. I guessed I'd run across the clearing sooner or later. And I couldn't really get lost because it was an island.

It took about twenty minutes to get to the graveyard. When I stepped out of the trees I knew Chief Copegog was there because it was cold. I yanked my sweater out of the pack and pulled it on. The graveyard looked almost peaceful — not scary at all. There were bars of sunlight slanting across the long grass and the birch saplings looked as if they were lit up. A lot of white butterflies were fluttering around and birds were chirping in the trees.

I looked around, holding the pack in my hand. Chief Copegog was in his usual place, perched up on the headstone, smoking a cigar. In that bright clearing, washed in sunlight, he looked pretty relaxed, like one of the old guys we see on the main street in town resting on benches at the bus stop. But there was something else. He looked sad slumped over and staring into the trees like that. I wondered if ghosts could feel loneliness and decided they must, because Chief Copegog looked the way I felt a lot of the time. I felt alone because I didn't have Kenny anymore to hang around with or to talk to. I tried to imagine how Chief Copegog must have felt, surrounded by the graves of friends and relatives.

And that's when I knew that, no matter how scary he looked, he couldn't be evil. He couldn't be like the horrible murdering ghosts in the movies who tear people to pieces or frighten them to death. I decided Noah must be right — a ghost was somebody sad, not bad.

So, hardly believing I could do it, I walked right up to him and said hello.

He turned to face me and blew out a big lungful of blue smoke. The red pin-point lights glowed fiercely in his black eyes' hollows.

"Figured you'd be back pretty soon," he said in his rough, faraway voice.

Then he smiled.

When he smiled, wrinkles creased the skin at the corners of his eyes and mouth. His cheekbones lifted and his slanty eyes practically closed. And with those spooky eyes almost closed, he looked almost human. He had yellowy teeth and a few of them were missing, making black squares in his smile. He was ugly, to tell the truth, but only in a magazine way — if you compared him to the hunks in the TV Guide and the fashion mags. His eyes still threw me off a little — not even a smile could warm up those deep black pits. But, in that sunny clearing, he wasn't terrifying. I wondered, could this be the same ghost that scared the life out of me last Friday night?

"Hi," I said again. "Hi, Chief Copegog." I

couldn't think of anything else to say, so I asked, "How do you like the cigars?"

"Pretty good, I guess." He looked at the glowing red end of the cigar, then at me. "This cigar, she's the last one."

"Oh," I said. Then I got his point. "I'd be glad to get you some more."

He nodded. He took a long drag on the cigar, pulled it out of his mouth, and blew the smoke in a thin stream up into the cold air.

"You're pretty small girl, but you got big problems."

"How do you know that?"

"Been around long time, I guess. Seen lotta sad little girls."

I decided there was no point in trying to lead up to what I wanted to say to him.

"How . . . do you mind if I ask you something?"

"That's okay."

"How come you're here?"

"I live this place."

"No, I mean, you're . . . you died, didn't you?"

"Yep. Long time back."

I felt stupid asking it. "So you're a ghost."

"I'm spirit now. Lost real body long time ago. Still can smoke these, though."

He took another long drag and sucked it deep into his lungs. Then he blew a couple of smoke rings and smiled, showing his yellow, stumpy teeth. His smile gave me confidence.

"What I'm wondering is, how come you're in . . . this life. I mean, I've never seen a ghost before." I thought of Noah's dad. "And most of the people I know don't even *believe* in ghosts."

When he talked, I noticed, he made his words

at the back of his mouth, sort of. And his S's sounded halfway between a whisper and a whistle.

"Spirit world is all around us. My peoples always knew that. Most peoples now, though, even this one —" he pointed to the freshly dug earth at my feet — "don't believe no more. My job, I got to lead the new dead peoples to the spirit world. Been doin' that long time, now. This one," he pointed to the fresh earth again, "I got to wait till he's ready to go across to the Other Side. Sometimes takes a while to let go this world."

"How did you get that job?" I felt like we were talking about a job pumping gas at the Canadian Tire twenty-four-hour gas bar.

He looked uncomfortable and a little embarrassed and stared off above the trees in the direction of the lake. I thought maybe I had asked something I shouldn't have, but he answered me.

He tugged at his earlobe. "Somethin' I did wrong when I was still 'live. Bad wrong. I got to pay for that."

So Noah was right, I thought. Chief Copegog was doing some kind of atoning, or whatever the word was.

He stuck the cigar into his mouth — it was pretty short by this time — and looked away into the trees as if someone had called him.

"Got to go now," he growled, getting down from the gravestone. He dropped the cigar stub onto the fresh earth.

"Wait! Please! I wanted to ask you something!"

I tried to grab his arm but my hand went through him, as if I had grabbed a handful of fog.

"I need to talk to you!" I shouted as he turned away. "Please stay!"

He turned back to face me. His face wasn't sad now. He looked like a kid does when he's done something really bad, and he's really sorry, and he feels . . . small. He wanted to go. I could see that, but I wanted him to stay. There was so much I wanted to ask him.

"You come back 'nother time, maybe," he said, and he started walking toward the trees, just like always. But before he got to them, he faded. Faded into nothing.

I stood there shivering for a minute, staring at the spot where he had been. I was so frustrated I could have screamed. But I just swore under my breath and stamped my foot. Then I turned and left the graveyard, stomping angrily across the rough ground in the slanting sunlight. The only sounds were the birds and the long dry grass swishing on my feet.

I got back to the rowboat without any problems, but I sure had problems when I got there. The northwest wind had come up like it often does at nightfall. There were waves out on the lake. And the wind had bashed the boat against the rocks and the bow was all scarred where the paint had been scraped off.

Oh, great, I thought, just what I need. Wait'll Dad sees *that*.

I tossed the pack into the bow and climbed in. I pulled on my life jacket, tied it, and started rowing, feeling really low, wondering if things were ever going to get better.

The boat lifted and fell as I rowed hard against the waves into the setting sun. The wind was blowing me down the lake as I went and my back and arms were already getting sore. I remembered what

my dad told John and me one time when we were
out fishing in the boat. I had hardly listened at the
time. He said that you should row and let the wind
move you down the lake as you went, then when
you got closer to shore you swung the bow right
into the wind and rowed straight. The main thing,
he said, was not to fight the wind because it would
always win.

I remembered that, and nothing terrible happened. By the time I got close to shore it was dark
and I had been blown way down the lake from our
house, past the park and the government dock. My
arms and shoulders felt like they were made of lead.
But all the lights from the buildings and the street
made it easy to see what I was doing. Through the
big windows of the Legion, I could see lots of people standing at the bar and crowding the tables and
laughing. A couple of guys were throwing darts.
Past the Legion, people were sitting out on the ter-
race of the seafood restaurant and there was cow-
boy music coming from the Champlain Hotel. The
liquor store was still open.

But I was rowing alone on the dark water. And
I was dead tired.

I steered the bow into the wind, which was a lot
lighter this close to shore, and rowed up the lake
toward our house. My shoulders and back were so
sore they were almost numb. I passed inside the
stone break wall near the government dock, past
the jetties sticking out into the water at all angles.

Soon I was passing the Couchiching Park beach
where the lifeguard towers were. I was so tired I
decided to pull in there and rest.

It was easy to row when I got close to the beach
because the wind was off shore. I clambered out

into the knee-deep choppy water, hauled the row-boat up onto the dry sand and walked up on shore. There were a few kids playing on the swings, a couple of dogs sniffing around the big maple trees, and a few people strolling around.

I walked past the swings and slides, across the road and onto the grass. I plunked myself down on the grass to rest, feeling a little silly, because from there I could have almost _seen_ our house if it hadn't been dark. Silly and sore. Every bone in my body ached and complained.

I glanced around and for the first time since I was really little I looked at the big shape looming above me in the dark, lit up by bluish floodlights. It was the monument, the big hunk of stone and bronze that, along with Stephen Leacock's old summer home, made Orillia famous. There was Samuel de Champlain, perched high on a grey stone slab, standing against the dark sky. He was dressed like one of the three musketeers, with a long flowing coat and one of those wide-brimmed hats in his hand, with a huge feather sticking out of it. His left hand was hooked in his wide belt and there was a long thin sword hanging at his side. He was wearing boots that came up to his knee. A pretty dashing figure, as Mom would have said. But he looked a little dumb standing on a rock down by the water as if he was guarding the swings so the little kids wouldn't have too much fun.

I got to my feet and walked up to the statue. I remembered from all the boring history we took that year that Sammy Dee, as we called him, had been a hot-shot French explorer in the 1600s and that he had come right past here. In fact, our teacher told us, there was a legend that he had lost an astrolabe right around here — one of those funny-looking things they used for navigation.

I always felt strange about all that stuff we learned in school, like how Sammy Dee discovered this and discovered that and how he claimed everything he saw for France. I couldn't figure out why the teacher said he discovered a place or a lake when the Indians knew it was there all along. I mean, they *lived* there. I talked to my dad about that and he agreed with me. He said that a bunch of the Ojibways from the Rama Reserve across the lake ought to pile into a pick-up truck and go down and "discover" Toronto and claim it for the band.

I walked around the statue. On the right side was a bald priest with a beard, wearing long robes. I remembered John had told me the Hurons had called the priests the Black Robes. This one was holding a cross up above his head and in his left hand he was holding a book — the Bible, I guessed. There were two almost naked Indians sitting at his feet on thick fur robes. They were sort of looking at the book, but not quite.

I walked around the back of the statue to the other side. There was a bronze fur trader standing there wearing a long coat, long pants and knee boots. He was holding a musket in his right hand and a string of beads in his left. There were two Indians sitting at his feet too, with fur robes across their knees, holding axes. I guessed that represented a trade.

I went around to the front of the statue and tried to read the bronze sign that was cemented into the stone.

1615-1915

Erected to commemorate the advent into Ontario of the white race under the leadership of Samuel de Champlain the intrepid French explorer and colonizer who with fifteen companions arrived in these parts in the summer of 1615 and spent the following winter with the Indians, making his headquarters at Chiague, the chief village of the Hurons, which was near this place.

A symbol of good will between the French and English speaking people of Canada.

How come the Indians got left out of the "good will," I thought. And I stood there wondering if Chief Copegog could see the Indians sitting at the feet of the white men, getting religion on one side and beads on the other while Sammy Dee watched the show. I hoped not.

I turned my back on Sammy Dee and dragged myself back to the rowboat. I pushed off from the beach, rowing with the waves till I got clear of the beach. Then I swung toward the house. As I hauled on the oars I was thinking. I was so mad I didn't feel tired anymore.

Late Monday Evening

I was lying on my waterbed, aching all over from my trip to the island, and frustrated because I hadn't had a chance to talk to Chief Copegog. I had taken a hot shower and changed into light cotton pajamas. It was about eleven o'clock and Minnie had been in the sack for half an hour.

I was reading *Anne of Green Gables* for the millionth time and I was at the part where Anne is floating down the river in the boat pretending she's Elaine, the Lily Maid, when I heard John and Noah clumping up the stairs. They went into John's room and turned the blaster on. A few minutes later I heard them coming down the hall to my room.

Knock on the door. Even though I knew it was them, I jumped. Boy, was I nervous.

"Yeah," I shouted, not too friendly.

"It's us. Can we come in? We've got some news."

Oh, no, I thought. News is one thing I don't

need. I've had enough "news" to last me a hundred years. I had already decided not to tell them about visiting the island that night.

But what could I say? If I told them to buzz off they'd be hurt.

I hauled myself off the waterbed, pulled on my housecoat and unlocked the door.

"Okay, come on in," I said, and went back to the bed.

John came in first, face shining like a little angel. His blue eyes sparkled the way they always do when he's turned on to something. His bands sparkled too, he was grinning so hard. He was still wearing his jogging shorts and tank top.

Noah looked pleased with himself too. His white T-shirt and black jeans were all wrinkled, as if he'd slept in them.

"We got it!" John announced like a guy on TV.

He and Noah were both carrying notebooks and Noah had a thick book that looked a million years old.

"Yeah," he said. "You're gonna love this, Karen. We found out who killed —"

"Wait!" John shrieked. "Let's tell it in order."

His voice sounded so silly I had to laugh. "John, can't this wait till —"

"No, no, you've got to hear this." He stepped across the room and settled on the window ledge.

Noah turned my desk chair around backwards and sat down, leaning forward against the chair back. The wedge of hair half covered his face.

"This is pretty hot stuff, Karen." He smiled. "We worked hard, and now —"

"Let's start at the beginning," John cut in.

"I know the beginning," I said. "All I don't know — and I'm not sure I want to — is who murdered the lawyer guy."

"Bond," Noah said.

"Whatever. So, who was it? Gimme a name so I can go to bed."

John looked hurt. "Aw, come on, Karen. What's the problem?"

Noah was looking straight into my eyes.

"Oh, nothing, I'm just tired. Go ahead, guys. Let's hear it."

"Okay," John said. "Tell her, Noah."

Noah looked surprised, but only for a second.

"Okay. Remember Bond was sort of the town creep, skating along on the edge of the law all the time?"

"Yeah."

"Built his house on land he cheated from an old lady client. Got his housekeeper's daughter pregnant. Probably got her into bed by promising to marry her. So she hanged herself, right? Then he had a record of getting hammered and beating up on the old guy who worked for him."

Noah paused and scratched the ear with the cross hanging from it. I thought of Chief Copegog, the way he pulled his big earlobe sometimes.

"So," John continued for Noah, dragging out his words, "somebody puts a blade through rich Mister Bond's hard, cold heart."

He smiled, pleased with himself.

"Yeah, right," I said. "His hard, cold heart. So who was it, the mother of the girl who hanged herself or the old man?"

"Guess again."

Noah groaned.

"All right, I will," I said, just to speed things up. "Um, let's see. The old man was beaten up a couple of times, isn't that what you guys told me before, Noah?"

"Right."

"Okay, then it probably wasn't him this time. I mean, why would he? Unless you're going to tell me the maid was his long-lost niece or something. Or that *he* was in love with the poor girl."

John shook his head.

"Or that — hey, wait! I know! The old man and the housekeeper were really secretly man and wife and the maid was their *daughter*! So that's why he did it."

Noah groaned again. "You're making this sound like a soap."

"*I'm* making it sound like a soap? Blame that on your research partner!" I pointed at John.

John ignored what I said. "So what's your guess, anyway?"

"The mother did it. Because Bond ruined her daughter's life and made her commit suicide."

"That's what *we* thought," Noah said.

John cut him off. "Until we really got into the records. That's when we found out about the Indian."

John was loving this. He had forgotten that he had asked Noah to be the storyteller. If I let him, he'd feed me bits of information the way you'd feed seeds to a canary and keep me going until I went out of my head.

"What Indian? Look, guys, I don't wanna rain on your parade, but why not just tell me straight out. With no games and suspense."

Noah nodded. He had his calm grown-up voice

back. "She's right, man. Just lay it out for her."

John shifted his position on the window ledge. I could see his back reflected in the window, along with my bedroom, and I could see Noah sitting at my desk. John nodded, then ran his hand through his almost-blonde hair.

"Okay, here goes. We were all wrong. I mean, totally. Bond was murdered by an Indian who got into the house one night, jabbed a knife into his cold" — John saw the scowl I pasted on my face — "okay, okay, his *heart*, and left him to bleed to death in the hall."

He pointed to my door. "Right out there."

My eyes followed his finger and a chill crept down my spine. I was glad the boys had shut the door on their way in.

John sat there saying nothing. I knew what I was supposed to say.

"Did they find out who did it?"

"Yeah," Noah said in a low voice. "The newspaper reports said the chief of the Ojibways did it."

"The thing is, Karen," John added, "the chief's name was Copegog."

An explosion went off in my head. I heard myself groan as I raised my hands to cover my face. This is never gonna end, I thought.

"We figure —"

I cut in on Noah. "I know what you figure."

"It's gotta be him," John said.

"Why does it have to be him?" I knew I was being stupid. Just like I knew what Noah was going to say before he said it.

"Remember I thought that when you opened the medicine bag you released a kind of power into the house and that's what triggered the poltergeist? Well, now we know. It's a real apparition. It's a ghost that's banging around here at night. We know whose ghost it is now. And we know who killed him. It must have been Chief Copegog, our friendly, cigar-smoking spirit. It was *his* medicine bag, and it brought out the ghost of the man *he* murdered."

I didn't want to believe it. How could the lonely old man whose spirit I saw be a murderer? Then I remembered the eyes. They were black and fierce, and they punched right through you like those pointed metal things they use to jab holes through leather.

I didn't *want* to believe it, though. My mind said it was logical. It made sense. But my heart refused to accept it.

Then I had a flash.

"Wait a sec," I said to John, "didn't you tell me that the new grave on Chiefs' Island was for a guy named Copegog? Isn't that the name you copied down?"

"Yeah, but —"

I turned to Noah. "And didn't you say he was the chief on the Reserve just before he died last week?"

"Sure. So what?"

"So this. There must have been *tons* of Chiefs over the years named Copegog. What's to say our ghost is the one who stabbed Bond the Creep? Who probably had it coming anyway."

Noah scrunched up his face and said, "Hmmmmm," then scratched his ear again. "Good point."

"Not so good," John said. "Because our guy is about the right age."

"How can you tell how old he is?" I said. Maybe this was going to work out, I thought.

But Noah smashed my hopes.

"Karen, remember what he said when I asked him how long it had been since he had a smoke?"

"Oh. Yeah, I get it. Wait! Maybe he had a brother who was chief too. That's possible."

"Get real, Karen." John sounded mad. I realized then that the two guys were probably almost as disappointed as I was. They wanted our ghost to be a friendly old Indian too, with lots of exciting stories about hunting and battles and stuff. Now he was just a murderer.

"Put everything together — his age, the medicine bag, when the ghost appeared here — it *must* have been him."

John slapped his leg, "And we went and bought him cigars!"

I didn't say anything. I didn't care anyway. I didn't.

"Well, I know what I think we should do to test this out," Noah said, standing up. "We should set up our equipment tonight and wait for the ghost to show up in the hall."

"Yeah, good idea," said John. Then he looked straight at me. "Maybe we'll find out we're wrong, Karen. Maybe we won't get anything, like last time. But it's worth a try, isn't it?"

I nodded.

"So let's go to my room and assemble all the

stuff. Do you have any empty audio tapes? We're gonna need lots. Maybe.''

"Yeah," I said tiredly. "I'll bring them in.''

After the guys left I thrashed around in the drawer of my desk and found a couple of cheap old tapes. I walked over to the window and pulled the curtains shut, almost knocking the glass bowl that had held Chief Copegog's medicine bag onto the floor. I didn't look out the window as I pulled the drapes shut.

When I turned to go to John's room I noticed that my closet door was open a little.

Wait a minute, I thought. I knew that it was closed and locked when I'd left for Chiefs' Island. Was it locked when I got home? I couldn't be sure. My mind had been on other things.

Who had been in there? John and Noah? It couldn't have been them. They'd left for the library before I'd left for the island. Unless — no, I wasn't even going to *think* about that.

I put the little hook in the little eye, shot a quick look at the silent wind chimes, left the room, and closed the door behind me.

I mostly stood around sulking and thinking while John and Noah set up the equipment. I must admit that after a few minutes of watching them I began to get into it. For one thing they looked so dumb. They looked like a couple of comedians, stumbling around, dropping tapes and wires, bumping into each other. Noah was fussing over the buttons on the machines and John the organizer wrote up a schedule for changing batteries and tapes. They were going to keep up the surveillance all night.

The video camera was perched on a tripod in the hall, pointed at my door.

"Anything that passes down the hall will be taped," Noah said.

I reminded him that the Sony hadn't recorded Chief Copegog but he ignored me. Boys always think girls don't know anything about machines.

At the top of the stairs they put a little portable tape recorder, one of those ones that has the mike right inside. They put another one right outside my room.

"That's where all the action has been," John reminded us. "So we got the video aimed there and we got sound there."

John wanted to sprinkle talcum powder all over the floor so footprints would show up.

"You mean *preternatural* footprints," I sneered.

"Oh, shut up, Karen."

Noah and John argued about whether footprints would show up in white powder. Noah said in all the stuff he had read about ghosts, he'd never heard of that. I said Skinny Minnie would have a heart attack and foam at the mouth if she saw powder all over the hall and that she'd tell Mom and Dad and they would ask a lot of questions and unless the guys wanted to tell Mom and Dad that we thought we were ghostbusters we better not do it.

The guys agreed.

The next thing we argued about was that they wanted to wait in my room for Bond the Creep's ghost to show up.

"No chance," I said. "I wanna go to bed."

I did too. I was dead tired and I wanted to sleep. My body still ached all over from the rowing. Sitting around waiting with those guys would drive me nuts.

"You're gonna *sleep*?" John asked.

"I'm gonna try."

So they set up shop, with their new batteries and their stacks of tapes and their time schedules, in John's room. I went into my room and shut the door.

And locked it.

I checked the closet door again — locked. I went over to the big bay window, pulled the curtains open, and sat on the ledge, pressing my face against the glass. The moon was almost hidden by clouds and Chiefs' Island was almost invisible — just a dark blurry shape out there.

Sure hope it wasn't you who did it, Chief Copegog, I said to myself.

I wondered if he was sitting on the gravestone waiting for me to bring him more White Owls. Then I thought I could feel those fierce eyes on me, and I stood and shut the curtains.

I felt sad and afraid at the same time. Why couldn't things be simple so I could understand them?

I pulled off my housecoat and dropped it on the floor. I turned on the reading light over my bed, then I snapped off the overhead light.

My room instantly became a dark cave with a little pool of yellow light where the waterbed was. I looked at the closed door. There was a thin line of light under it.

I sighed and climbed into bed. I didn't even try to read, just snuggled down deep and closed my eyes and waited for the ghost to start its show.

I didn't have long to wait.

day five

Early Tuesday Morning

I was deep inside a real bad dream when the noises started. In the dream I was dressed in an old-fashioned Dracula-movie nightgown again and I was sort of floating through a graveyard, out of control, as if I was hypnotized. The graveyard was misty and silvery with moonlight and the gravestones glowed as if they were alive. There was a low dark shape slinking along beside me and I knew it was a werewolf. The moonlight glistened on its long teeth.

Ahead I could see an old Indian with piercing red eyes and a necklace made of animal teeth and a long, wicked-looking knife in his hand.

The werewolf raised its head and there was terror in its green eyes. It turned around slowly and melted away between the graves. Then I heard what scared it. A tinkling sound, like bits of glass clinking together.

When I woke up I knew I had awakened into another nightmare. I could still hear the tinkling sound. It was the wind chimes. My bedroom was freezing and my breath made frost clouds that puffed into the pool of yellow light my bed lamp threw onto the waterbed.

I sat up, leaning back against the wall, and gathered the blanket around me, staring at the door. Waiting. The tinkling of the wind chimes faded to silence.

Then it came — the pounding, the noise that had awakened me. It started as a strong knock, like someone with big hands wanted to get in. But the pounding got louder and harder, almost desperate. The door shook and rumbled so hard I thought it would fly out of the frame.

Then dead silence. No jangle from the wind chimes. No banging. Only the harsh rasp of my breathing.

The door handle turned slowly, first one way, then another. I shivered, not just from the cold.

Whoever was on the other side of my door trying to get in seemed angry that the handle wouldn't work, because the knob started to rattle like crazy and the pounding shook the door again.

It stopped.

I took a deep breath and let out a long sigh. Maybe that was the end —

Something scratched around the bottom of the door!

I heard myself gulp down a cry. Maybe this time the ghost *would* come in. I had a crazy thought. I wondered if ghosts could bleed. Would Bond's blood drip and splash onto my rug?

But I heard a laugh and footsteps ran away down the hall. They stopped dead. Silence. Laughter again. The footsteps ran back toward my room but turned into the bathroom.

I heard someone rummaging around in there, opening the medicine chest, moving bottles around. Something fell and smashed on the floor. The medicine chest door banged shut and the footsteps ran back into the hall. The laugh came again.

And that's when I realized something was very wrong.

I had been too scared and shocked to notice it before. That wasn't a grown-up's laugh! And the more I thought about it, the more convinced I was that the running and the footsteps weren't like a man's either.

The sounds of walking around in the hall kept going for a few more minutes. Then, *click, click, click.* Back and forth. Something being dragged on the wooden floor, *click, click, click*, up the hall to the stairs, back toward my door. A while later, *Thump! Thump! Thump!*

Last, the skittering laugh as the footsteps ran down the hall toward the stairs.

Soon after that the wind chimes gave one last jangle and the room began to warm up. I knew the poltergeist had gone.

I fell sideways on my bed, exhausted. Every muscle I owned had been held stiff and tight — from the cold and from fear. I slid down under the blanket and tried to drift off into sleep.

No luck, though. A few minutes later, the banging on my door came back. But this time it sounded *normal*. I knew it was the boys. I got up, put on my housecoat and went to the door.

John had on those goofy yellow polo pajamas

— the ones with tight cuffs and ankles — and his slippers. Noah was wearing jeans and no shirt.

They looked excited and a little spooked.

"Did you hear him?" John blurted out. He looked at my face and added, "Dumb question."

Noah was all business. "Karen, did anything out of the ordinary happen?"

I shot him a sarcastic look and he added, "Anything different, I mean?"

"Yeah, it went into the bathroom this time."

"The *bathroom*?"

"Who ever heard of a ghost taking a pee?" John said, and laughed at his own joke. I was so keyed up I laughed too.

"Okay, let's check the equipment," said Noah, ignoring him.

John led us out into the hall. We moved quietly and whispered so we wouldn't wake Skinny Minnie up. All three of us noticed what was wrong right away.

The cassette had been taken from the tape recorder near my door and the thin brown tape pulled from it. The tape lay on the floor in a tangled, curly mess. The batteries had been taken out too. They were sitting on the hardwood, four of them, lined up in a neat row, the labels facing in the same direction.

"It's mocking us," Noah said. "Well, that makes sense. A poltergeist *is* playful."

The red light still glowed on the video recorder, showing it was still on. Noah was checking it out when we heard him cry, "Hey! What's this?"

"Shhhhhhhhh!" John hissed. "Skinny Minnie might hear you!"

All three of us held still, listening, staring at the door that led to Minnie's room above the garage. It never occurred to us that the ghost's racket would have wakened her. Anyway, her door was closed.

John and I stepped up to Noah, who pointed to the lens of the camera. Some tan-coloured goo was smeared all over the glass. No way was that thing taking any pictures now.

"Looks like your pimple cream," I said to John.

"Very funny."

I noticed a squashed-up tube on the floor beside one of the tripod legs and picked it up. Sure enough, it *was* John's pimple cream. I handed it to him, smiling.

"Must have got it from the bathroom," he murmured. "This sure is weird."

The tape recorder at the top of the stairs was messed up just like the one outside my room.

"I guess all we can do is see if the camera picked up anything before it was tampered with," Noah said. He went to the camera and took out the cassette.

A few minutes later we were in the dark living room huddled in front of the TV watching a still picture of the upstairs hall.

"Hey, I just thought of something," Noah whispered, not moving his eyes from the screen.

"Mmmm?" I said.

"Well, listen. Bond the Creep died way over a hundred years ago, right?"

"Right," John answered.

"So, don't you get it?" Noah still had his eyes glued to the TV. He didn't intend to miss anything. "His ghost wouldn't know what a tape recorder *is*!

Or a video camera!''

"Yeah, so?" John tore his gaze from the screen and looked at Noah.

"So how would he know how to screw them up? I mean, he wouldn't even know what they *are*."

Something clicked in my brain, but I didn't say anything.

"Oh. Yeah. Well, I guess he . . . learned about them." John laughed. "He hasn't had much to do for all these years."

"No way, man. Ghosts are frozen in the time frame they died in. They can't go back to school."

"Yeah, I see what you mean. But —"

"Look!" I cut in. "Something moved!"

"Yeah, I saw it too!" Noah said.

On the TV screen a sort of grey shape came into view, then disappeared.

"Rewind it," said John. "Let's see it again."

"No, wait, let's let it run," Noah answered.

The shape came back. It wasn't the shape *of* anything. It certainly wasn't what you'd call a *human* shape.

But the hand was.

It was grey, too, mist-coloured, and small. It sort of *appeared* in front of the camera, palm facing us. A little hand, not a grown-up's. It came closer and closer to the camera, then it disappeared and the lights almost went out.

"That's the goo he put on the lens we're seeing," said Noah. "We won't see any more."

He reached over and pressed the rewind button, then the play button.

He and John watched the grey shape and the hand over and over.

I didn't.

Because I was filled with a feeling I couldn't describe. A mixture of terror and . . . and *hope*.

Everything started to make sense now. The sounds outside my bedroom door, the shape, the hand. Everything.

Before I knew what I was doing I jumped to my feet and started running.

"Karen, where —"

"The study!" I shouted. I didn't care who heard me now. "The sounds in the hall! He was running for the study!"

The two guys were right on my heels when I got to my dad's drafting table and clicked on the lamp.

There on the table the charcoal sticks were broken and scattered. And there was a single piece of paper, with the marks drawn in charcoal.

The fear-hope feeling was like a burning inside me, filling me up. Snatching the paper from the table I ran for the stairs and flew up them two at a time.

"Karen! What's the matter?" John shouted from behind me. He sounded terrified.

I ignored him and tore down the hall and burst into my room, slamming the door back against the wall. I flipped on the light, grabbed my chair, and dragged it to the closet. The little hook hung uselessly. The closet was unlocked.

Throwing open the door, I shoved the chair inside and climbed up onto it. I grabbed the brass box, jumped off the chair and carried it to the desk.

"Karen, what's going on?" Noah asked, his voice tense. "Tell us."

I got down on my hands and knees and snatched the key from its hiding place, not caring now if the guys knew about it. I unlocked the big heavy padlock and dropped it onto the desk. My fingers trembled as I grabbed the lid.

I raised the lid of the box and carefully lifted out Kenny's stuff — the slingshot, the pocket watch on the long thick chain, the pink skateboard wheels and chunk of painted wood, the photo.

There was nothing left inside.

The red, white and blue striped ball was missing. I remembered one of the sounds I had heard in the hall — *thump, thump, thump* — a ball bouncing! And the plastic toy airplane with the little pilot inside was missing too. When you dragged the toy along, the pilot's head snapped from side to side. And the wheels went *click, click, click*.

I began to laugh and cry at the same time, going crazy. My voice rose higher and higher like a siren.

"I know who it is! I know who the ghost is!"

"Karen, stop it!"

I snatched up the paper from the study and practically threw it at John.

"Look! Hold it up in front of the mirror." I could feel myself getting hysterical. I was getting out of control. But I didn't care. *It was all clear now.*

"It's Kenny!" I screamed. "It's Kenny! It's Kenny! The ghost is Kenny!"

16

Tuesday Morning

The three of us spent the rest of the night talking. I sat on my bed with my legs tucked under me and the blanket gathered around me. A box of kleenex sat on the pillow and used tissues lay scattered around me like lumps of snow. John had pulled my desk chair over to the foot of the bed. Noah sat Indian-style on the rug. He had put his T-shirt on inside out and hadn't noticed yet. Neither had John.

It took John and Noah a while to get me calmed down, and when they did I broke down and cried for a long time. It was like something I had been keeping inside, fighting to keep deep in the darkness, had burst out into the light. I couldn't stop the tears. I didn't *want* to.

I had to argue pretty hard, too, sniffing and blowing my nose the whole time, because at first they wouldn't buy the idea that the poltergeist or "preternatural event" or whatever they wanted to call it was Kenny's ghost — not even after I held the sheet of paper up to the mirror. John held out as long as he could. He didn't want it to be Kenny. When he realized he couldn't pretend anymore his face sort of crumpled and got red and he started to cry too.

When that happened I got off the bed and hugged him and I could feel the big sobs tossing around inside his skinny body like waves. I knew how he felt. All the pain from losing his little brother had come back. Finally, when John had settled down a bit, he looked up at me. His face was streaked with tears and his nose was running. His hair stuck out in all directions. He didn't look like John.

"I miss him," he said.

I bent down and hugged him again. "You don't need to miss him any more," I said. "He's back!"

"He can't be back! He can't be!" John burst out as he pushed me away. "He's . . . he's *dead*, Karen!"

I sat back down on the waterbed and turned to Noah. "You believe he's back, don't you?"

Noah leaned over, resting his elbows on his knees, and looked at the floor. His long black hair covered his face.

"Um, I don't know, Karen. I mean, what you're saying sounds pretty weird, even to me."

He looked up at me and the hair fell away to show half his face. Water stood out in his eyes.

"I don't want to hurt you any more than you are already," he said softly, "but Kenny *died*, Karen. Maybe you never really accepted that — you know, *dealt* with it. Even if the poltergeist *is* him, it's an apparition, not a real person. You gotta face that."

"What do you know about it?" I snapped.

"You've never lost anybody!"

Noah looked straight into my eyes. "Yes, I have," he said quietly.

I thought of the picture in his room, hanging over his bed, and I felt bad for what I had said.

"Haven't you seen her since she left?"

Noah looked at the floor again and sniffed. "Nope. She calls every Sunday, though, when she knows *he* is in church, giving one of his stupid sermons. She's in Edmonton. Someday," he said in a hard, determined voice, "I'm going out there and not coming back."

"I'm sorry, Noah, for what I said."

He looked up and gave me a weak smile. "That's okay. You're right in a way. I guess I haven't really *lost* her, but it feels like it at times — most of the time, actually. I don't know *what* I'd do if she died, like Kenny."

"You *know* it's him, don't you, Noah?"

Noah heaved a big sigh and nodded. "Yeah, Kenny's here all right. At first I figured the Chief's medicine bag released the power stored up inside the house by Bond. He was a really tough personality with a strong life force. When we found out about the murder, it all fit — or seemed to. The medicine bag belonged to the guy who killed Bond. I don't think there's any doubt about that. But, yeah — some of the noises you described, and the running and laughing, and the marks made with the charcoal — they don't fit with Bond. They're too *playful*."

"Right. They're all kid stuff."

Noah ran his fingers through his hair and fiddled with the cross hanging from his ear for a moment. He turned and looked at the door.

"On the other hand, that pounding and banging on the door seems too angry, too *violent*. I don't know, Karen, maybe —"

"Maybe what?"

Noah turned back and gave me a long look, then said, "Nothing. Nothing. We know Kenny's here. That's the main thing. Right?"

I sniffed and wiped the tears away for the millionth time.

"Do you think Kenny wants to get a message to us?"

"Yeah, I guess that's a possibility. He could be just playing, you know. Remember, that's what poltergeist means. And another thing, Karen. You better realize that he could stop any time."

"You mean he won't stay?" John cut in.

"I don't know. But ghosts are funny. Sometimes they turn up for a while and then all of a sudden they just stop appearing. Sometimes they hang around forever almost. We just don't know."

"I wonder why he didn't appear to Mom and Dad," John said, almost to himself. "They miss him too. I know they do."

"That's easy. Adults are too realistic — most of them, anyway. And besides, Karen is his twin. From what you told me, they were especially close."

I shot a look at John. I was surprised he had talked to Noah about me.

"So what should we do?" asked John.

Noah let out a big yawn and pushed his hair back from his face. "I don't know, John. To tell you the truth, I'm too tired to think. This has been some night."

"I know what we should do. I know who we should talk to about this."

John looked at me. "I don't know about that, Karen. I think we should stay away from there."

"No way. I'll ask him to help us. John, I *know* he's not a bad guy. I know it. I don't care what you and Noah found out or didn't find out in the library, I don't think he'd hurt us."

Noah said, "You remember the first time I went with you guys to see him? He said something to you, Karen. Do you remember?"

John and I nodded at the same time.

"Well, I think he's got a special interest in you. And I agree — he wouldn't hurt us."

John shrugged his shoulders. "Well, it's worth a try, I guess."

John got up and went to the desk. His yellow polo pajamas were all wrinkled. He picked up Kenny's watch and looked at it. Then he turned to me. The look on his face broke my heart.

"I wish he hadn't come back," he said in a shaky voice. Tears ran down his face.

"Why?" I shot back. "Why not?"

"Because when . . . if he goes, it'll be like we lost him *twice*! I don't think I could stand that."

"He isn't going to go away again," I said softly. "I won't let him."

Before he left my bedroom Noah gave me a strange look.

After the boys left I lay back and covered my eyes with my arm. My mind started to replay pictures of my twin brother Kenny. The pictures were like short scenes cut from a movie.

I saw him on a hot summer day playing in the dark cool boathouse. He was five. He was wearing white shorts with blue stripes down the sides. He was barefoot and had tossed his T-shirt carelessly onto the dock. His short chubby body was a rash of freckles. He had caught a few spotted leopard frogs along the lakeshore where the reeds and lily pads were and put them in a bait bucket. The silver-coloured bucket hung below the water, tied to a ring bolt on the dock with a piece of the twine Mom used to tie her tomato plants.

Then I saw him playing pirates in there when he was seven, all by himself, jumping in and out of the rowboat with a wooden sword in his hand and a white hankie folded to make a headband to hold down his blazing red hair, shrieking orders to his imaginary crew and threats to the imaginary enemy. The boathouse was where he and I first tried smoking. We coughed a lot and then threw the cigarette into the water and forgot all about it.

In another picture, Kenny stood on the dock, holding a string with both hands. He was ten. He was wearing jeans and a Hillcrest T-shirt. His body was bent to the side from the weight of the big pike on the end of the string. The proud grin on his face was huge. Dad knelt on the dock, a camera held up to his eye.

All summer when we were little kids we used to play in the tree house in the weeping willow by the lake. The long hanging branches made a cave that shut out the rest of the world. We played school and we played house. Kenny played with my dolls without complaining. When we got older we'd act out scenes from *Jacob Two-Two and the Hooded Fang or Anne of Green Gables*. The willow tree was where we always went if something was wrong or if we wanted to be alone together.

These mental pictures of the willow tree reminded me of the time Kenny and I and some kids from the neighbourhood were playing hide-and-go-seek and I was "It." I guess we were about six. It was autumn, I remembered — the trees had turned. There were a few kids from the neighbourhood playing with us and I was counting, my forehead pressed against the rough bark of one of the maples on our front lawn, my eyes squeezed shut. "Eighty, ninety, a HUN-DRED!" I counted and opened my eyes. I walked carefully along the cedar hedge that separated our front yard from the street, looking in and under the hedge. I turned and walked across the lawn, peered around the corner of the house, and headed for the back yard. Behind me I heard Jannie Baker shout, "Home Freeeeeee!" Suddenly I got an image in my mind of Kenny sitting on the big branch that jutted out of the willow tree a few feet from the ground. Even though the branch was low, the hanging branches and leaves hid it from view. But in my mind I could "see" Kenny sitting on it in the gloom, trying to peer through the yellowed leaves to see if I was coming. I ran back to the front of the house and slapped the maple "home" tree shouting, "One, two, three on Kenneeeee!"

After that day we found out that Kenny could see pictures in his head of me sometimes too. But we never told anyone, not even Mom or Dad.

A year or so later we discovered that, not only could we send each other messages when we weren't together (which wasn't very often), we could also sort of "talk" when we were in the same room without looking at each other and without saying anything. Like if I went into the kitchen to get a glass of milk I would know if Kenny wanted one too without asking him. One time in grade five we cheated on a test when I didn't know how to do an arithmetic question and Kenny did. He "sent" me the answer and I got perfect on the test. We didn't do that too much, though. Only when we had to.

Another picture began to form in my mind, slowly, like a backwards dissolve. I tried to fight it down. I opened my eyes and looked over to the brass-covered box on my desk. The astrology figures on the brass glowed softly in the light — the Bear, the Scorpion.

The Gemini.

My mind drifted as my heavy eyelids began to close against my will. The picture began to backwards dissolve again. I fought it, pushed it down, but I couldn't stop it.

Kenny stood in the pool of cool shade under the willow branches, holding his new street board by the front truck.

Karen! Karen! Lookit! I can do a Simon Sez . . .

17

Tuesday Afternoon: Chiefs' Island

We got to the town docks at about noon. John had his back pack on, Noah was carrying his electronic gear in his bigger pack, and I had three boxes of White Owl cigars.

Noah had on his black denim cut-offs and a black T-shirt that had a picture of a plate with knife and fork on either side of it and EAT THE RICH in big white letters on top. John wore long pants and a long-sleeved shirt. He was convinced we'd be attacked by mosquitoes once we got to Chiefs' Island and he wanted to be prepared. I was wearing my track suit again. I was hot, but if we found Chief Copegog it would get cold *fast*.

We were going to use Noah's uncle's little aluminum fishing boat, but Noah's uncle didn't know that. Noah had come up with the idea. He said the boat could get us to the island in ten minutes.

We left Skinny Minnie all set up in the front yard,

sprawled in a lounge, with a pitcher of Kool Aid, a giant bag of cheezies, two Harlequin Romances, the *National Enquirer*, and John's ghetto blaster. Her narrow body glistened with suntan oil. When I told her we were going for a walk she just grunted and turned a page.

"There's the boat, down at the end of the dock," said Noah.

The little boat bobbed in the waves that rolled against the dock from a passing cabin cruiser. We stepped down into it and Noah hooked up the black gas hose to the motor and squeezed the bulb on the hose. Then he pulled out the choke and yanked on the starter cord. The little Evinrude coughed a little, then started roaring. The boat vibrated with the noise.

John and I untied the ropes and we were on our way.

It was pretty hot out and a lot of boats were on the lake. Kids were water skiing, kicking up rooster tails behind the skis. A few canoes were slipping along. We chugged past the park where old Sammy Dee was perched on his hunk of stone.

When we got to Chiefs' Island we landed at a different spot. John thought we should try to get to shore without anyone seeing us, so we sneaked into a little bay and turned off the motor and waited until things were quiet. Then we got out and waded in to shore. It was harder to pull the boat up than it was to beach our rowboat because of the motor, but it was no big deal.

"Come on, let's go," I said as soon as we had the boat out of sight in the trees.

"Yeah, yeah, hold your horses," John answered. "We gotta get our gear."

He dug the bug dope out of his pack and tossed it to me.

"Better put lots on, Miss Impatience. Bugs'll be thick today."

While I smeared the dope on, Noah was getting his gear ready. He hung the tape recorder around his neck and switched it on. He mumbled to the recorder while he got the video camera ready.

"Noah, how come you brought that again? It didn't work before."

He looked at me through the camera lens. "You never know. We got Kenny on tape — or at least his hand. So maybe Chief Copegog can let himself appear on tape if he wants. This is new ground we're breaking here. None of the stuff I've read about the supernatural mentions video."

"Well, how about the cross? Want me to carry it?"

"Didn't bring it this time."

"How come?"

"I don't know. I didn't think we'd need it."

Finally we were ready. "Let's get going," I said.

"No, wait." Noah looked embarrassed. "I forgot to put on any mosquito lotion."

I groaned. Noah took off all his gear and stood there with it piled at his feet as he rubbed on the dope. Then he slung the equipment onto his body again and we started out.

Once we got moving it only took about twenty minutes to get to the graveyard.

It was hot in the clearing. The sun beat down on the gravestones and the long grass was dry and wilty. The leaves on the birches hung down, tired-looking. There was no breeze.

Chief Copegog was nowhere to be seen.

I heard John swear under his breath, so I knew he was as disappointed as I was. He let his pack slip off his back onto the ground and leaned on the gravestone with the new letters carved into it.

"You think it's too early?" he said. "I mean, maybe he doesn't like the bright sun."

"Search me," said Noah. "I got an idea, though. Karen, toss me one of those boxes of White Owls." He handed the camera to John. John started photographing everything. And I mean everything — the sky, his feet, everything.

I did what Noah asked. He pulled the thin red tape on the top of the box and stripped off the cellophane. He stuffed it into the pocket of his jeans. He opened the box and drew out a fat brown cigar. It was wrapped in cellophane, too.

"You know, I got a theory," he said as he unwrapped the cigar. "In our society we like wrapping better than what comes in it. I mean, look at —"

"Come *on*, Noah, get *on* with it!" I cut in.

"Okay, okay," he said, lighting the cigar.

His face screwed up as he puffed a few times. The foul-smelling smoke rolled out of his mouth and sort of floated around us. The sunlight seemed to light it up, a blue-grey layer. It looked pretty and smelled terrible.

We waited for a few minutes, looking around, peering into the quiet forest. We saw nothing and heard only birds.

"Where's the wind when we need it?" John said.

"I guess this isn't our day," Noah sighed. "Let's put the gear away, John. Might as well save the batteries."

Noah put the cigar down on the gravestone and

shrugged off his pack. While he and John put the gear into the pack I picked up the cigar and put the end in my mouth. I puffed hard. A horrible, bitter taste filled my mouth as the blue-grey smoke floated around my head and I started to cough like crazy. Tears rolled down my cheeks. I felt dizzy.

"Figured it was you kids."

I don't know what surprised me more — the rough, faraway voice — I knew right away whose it was — or the sudden cold. I mean, it was *instant*.

I waved the smoke away, trying to see. Sure enough, Chief Copegog was standing behind John and Noah.

He had on the same skin pants and vest, and his medicine bag dangled from his waist. His fierce eyes seemed to bore right through me, but he was smiling, his slanted eyes almost closed. I wasn't scared.

"I — we — were afraid you wouldn't be here," I said.

"Here all the time," he answered. "Never wander far from this place."

"What did you say, Karen?" John said.

"Hey! It's cold," Noah said excitedly. "Feel it? He must be close."

Noah and John began to look around. John snapped the camera up to his eye and waved it back and forth like a winkie.

"Did you smell the cigar smoke?" I asked.

"Yep. Knew you were here anyway, though."

"Oh, yeah, I guess you did."

"Karen, what are you *talking* about?" John sounded scared. He lowered the Sony.

I shifted my eyes to the boys. John was staring at me with his mouth open and Noah kept looking back and forth between John and me, looking really confused.

"Can you let them see you?" I asked him.

"Don't really want to talk to them."

"Please," I said. "John's my brother and Noah's my friend."

"Noah, we gotta get her out of here. I think she's flipped her lid. I knew we shouldn't have —"

"Wait. There's something weird going on, man. Can't you feel the cold?"

"Yeah, I can. Sure I can," John answered. "But —"

"I think he's here," Noah interrupted. Then to me he said, "Karen, can you see him?"

"He's here, Noah."

"You still got lots troubles, don't you girl?" said the Chief. He walked between the boys and came up to me and held out his hand. The palm was creased and wrinkled like tough leather. I knew what he wanted. I gave him the cigar. He took a long, deep drag and the smoke poured from his nostrils.

"You kids, you're pretty kind," he said as he hiked himself up onto the gravestone. "Yep, you're good kids."

"He's *where*?" John cried out. Then, "I see him!"

"Me, too!" said Noah. "Hi, Chief Copegog."

The Chief nodded to the boys and took another puff.

"Um," Noah began, "how come you didn't appear to all of us at once?"

The Chief shrugged and looked off into the trees. I was afraid when he did that. Every other time he'd done that he'd disappeared. I figured I'd better get down to why I had come.

"Chief Copegog," I began, and my voice creaked. I cleared my throat and started again. "Chief Copegog, I came here to talk to you about something that's very important and you're the only one who can help me."

"Yep, you got troubles all right. Too many troubles for little girl like you."

I had a thought. "Did you . . . before . . . did you have any kids?"

He took the cigar out of his mouth and some of the fierce spookiness disappeared from his eyes.

"Had lots of kids," he said in a low voice. "All gone now."

"Where?" I said. "Where did they go?"

"Karen," John broke in, "that's a stupid quest —"

I shushed him. I could hear Noah rustling around in his pack as I said, "Can you tell me?"

Chief Copegog looked at me. I could see the sadness in his face, like last time. I imagined him as a grandpa sitting beside a fire, surrounded by five or six fat little Indian kids shrieking and playing.

"Was my fault," he said so low I could hardly hear him. "That's why I got to pay."

"How? Pay for what?"

"I got to lead the spirits from the band to the Other Side. But me, I can't go that place. I got to keep doin' this until I paid."

The cigar between his thick fingers burned forgotten as he stared into the trees. It was like he could see something out there. What did he mean? I thought. I couldn't fit it together and I was afraid to ask too much in case he left us again. I decided I had to try, though.

"Did you . . . did you have a daughter like me?"

He shifted his gaze from the trees to my face and coughed. His voice was thick when he answered.

"Had lots of kids," he said again. "Two kids like you, 'bout your age, maybe little younger. Girl and a boy. Born same time, same minute almost. Looked same. Them kids, they was my favourites. Special to the spirits, see? Because they was born same minute. Can't see them now, 'cause I can't go the Other Side."

Twins! Chief Copegog had had twin kids!

Behind me I heard John whisper, "Karen, ask him —"

"Please tell me some more," I said softly.

He looked into my eyes and seemed to make a decision. He hopped off the gravestone and for a second, panic hit me. I thought he was going to leave. But he just lowered himself to the ground, leaning back on the gravestone, and sat in its shadow with his legs crossed.

I sat down in front of him on the fresh earth, the same way. John sat on my right and Noah moved around and sat on my left. We formed a half circle in front of him with the gravestone behind. It was still very cold, but I noticed it wasn't as bad as before. It didn't seem to go *into* me.

When Chief Copegog began to talk his voice changed. Now it was softer, like wind in long grass. And there was a sort of rhythm to it, halfway between speaking and chanting.

"When my brother went to Other Side I became Chief of the band. We lived all 'round here.

Weren't stuck on damn Reserve like my peoples now. Had lotta problems, them days. Game and fish disappearing. Whites coming in more and more. Had to decide. Stay and live with Whites or go back north, northwest into the land where Whites didn't go so much.

"Lotta Elders in the band wanted to go back. I thought, okay, be good for coupla years, then same problem. Some day we got to stop runnin'.

"So one time, I went to that place, York, to take good look at the White world. Travelled southeast long way by water until the big lake, then west. Terrible place, that York. Could smell it day before I finally got there. Full of ugly wood buildings — tall too. Big iron boats with black smoke comin' out, wagons with them big ugly horse animals, mud and smoke. People runnin' 'round. Not goin' anywheres.''

Chief Copegog paused and puffed his cigar. It had gone out while he talked. Noah quickly struck a match and leaned forward to hold the flame to the end of the cigar.

It looked so strange — an old Indian wearing skin clothes and a headband and a medicine bag, having his cigar lit by a kid with worn cut-offs and a T-shirt, with the sides of his head buzzed and a cross dangling from his ear. Then it hit me. What was the big difference? I knew that Indian men used to decorate themselves and put stuff in their hair. John had lectured to me about all that enough times. Kids I knew did all that too. The decorations were different now, that was all.

The Chief smiled sadly at Noah and took a long drag on the White Owl. Beside me, John began to whisper.

"York, that's what Toronto was called back then, Karen." Then a strange look came over his face. He gulped and said, "And I think around that time the cholera —"

"I knew then when I saw that ugly place," Chief Copegog went on, "no one could stop them Whites. Thought about it all the way back to the band. My mind, she was split in two. Hated that ugly York, but it showed me we couldn't stop them Whites. Decided I would try to get the Elders to go along with me. We had to stay and try to live with the Whites. Maybe we didn't hafta go the White men's way, but we had to live with 'em.

"So the band, she moved from this place to Narrows. Built some wood lodges like Whites had, built a school, a church.

"Trouble was, that sickness came. Many of the peoples was sick and many others went away into the hills north to get away from the sickness. All my family but me had the sickness.

"Lotta peoples died that time."

He stopped talking and stared into the trees. I realized then that when he looked away like that he was looking into the past, seeing all his kids and his wife sick, lying on beds in strange houses, close to death.

"I went into the town to talk to the govmint agent fella 'bout a treaty. Had big house, that guy. Still there, I guess. Fella name Bond."

Noah shot me a quick look and I heard John catch his breath. Inside me, tension began to squeeze like a cold fist.

"Talked to that guy long time, day after day. Explained what the peoples needed — lotta land without no White boats or machines or stone buildings. Lotta land for trapping, hunting.

"That guy, he promised me all kinds things. Said he was White Father sent by govmint to take care of us Ojibway children. Said the band would get evrythin' I asked. I just hadda make a mark on a paper.

"I tol' him I gotta talk with the Elders 'bout all that. That's the Indian way. The peoples gotta agree. He said I could mark the paper, come back tomorrow, I was Chief. I said no, gotta have a council.

"Went back to the band. Couldn't find some Elders. They was gone into the hills, north. My wife and my kids, they was worse. Sick real bad. My heart was achin' for them. Couldn't do nothin' for them, their sufferin', 'cept wait and see if they was stronger than the bad sickness-spirit.

"Next day I went an' tol' Bond I couldn't sign. Had to wait for sickness to pass and Council could get back together. He got real mad. Then, little later, Bond tol' me he could get strong medicine for the peoples, White medicine, would chase the sickness away."

Chief Copegog paused and cleared his throat.

"But I had to mark the paper first."

John groaned and swore and shook his head. Noah dropped his head and his long black hair fell across his face.

"I tol' him I would talk to Elders. I would find them in the hills, one by one, talk to 'em, if he would give the medicine. He said No, mark the paper first."

The Chief was looking at the ground too. He was

talking almost in a whisper, so that his voice seemed to come from a hundred years away.

"So I did that thing he wanted. Took a big feather with black water on the end and marked a paper. Made a scratchy sound, that feather. Then Bond, he gave me a cloth bag with brown powder in it. Had strong smell, that powder. Said boil some powder in water, get sick peoples to drink it. Sickness be driven away.

"I went back to the home place fast as I could. Gave out the powder to my family and the peoples there and later took some into the hills to find rest of my peoples. Was gone three days.

"Came back to the home place and my kids was dead. Wife was dead. Found them all in the wood lodge, all swelled up, with tongues hangin' out. Bad smell there, too.

"My heart sneaked away, then. Never came back."

The old man let out a long, painful sigh. When he started talking again, the rhythm speeded up.

"Same day, an Elder tol' me that medicine, that's no good. Said it was somethin' lotta Whites drank. Called it 'coffee.'

"And all the peoples was mad at me. Said White mens came, told 'em to get off that land. White land now. Told 'em we all hadda move across the lake. Waved a paper 'roun', called it Surrender Number 48, said it had my mark on it.

"Then I knew that Bond fella, he tricked me.

"Same night, I went 'cross the lake to talk to Bond, make him take back that paper. He laughed at me. Used an Indian word to me, bad word, meant I was lowest thing alive.

"I could see my kids' faces in front of me when I took out my knife and kilt that guy."

Chief Copegog stopped talking and cleared his throat again. He lifted his head. There were tears running down his wrinkled cheeks.

"I ran away into the bush after that. Nothin' to go home for. Lived alone in shame lotta years.

"One winter mornin' I was pushin' along a frozen river bank, checkin' the trapline. Snow was deep that winter, hard goin'. Big storm came up that day, blew in fast. Had to hole up to wait out the blizzard. Waited three days. I was sittin' in there in the dark, in my shelter, freezin'. Started thinkin' 'bout my family. Felt so bad I went out that place, walked into the wind's teeth. Laid down in a snowdrift and went to sleep.

"When I left this world, couldn't get into the next one. Now I got to lead the peoples there when their time comes, but I got to stay between. I'm outcast."

The cigar was cold in his hands. I noticed Noah flipping the tape over.

"But that wasn't your fault!" I said. "You did the best you could."

Chief Copegog frowned and shook his head. "That's White thinkin'. Indian way, we got to decide together. We're a band, all peoples fit, all got a place. Even crazy ones or sick ones or old ones. All got a place. I betrayed that, see? Decided on my own. 'Cause I wanted that medicine for my kids, specially them kids born same minute. Thought of myself, not my band. Now . . . "

He didn't finish the sentence.

Noah said, "Is your punishment . . . eternal?"

"I got to do this till I pay back the band. Sometimes outcast can get back in if he does somethin' special good."

I felt kind of selfish then about bothering Chief Copegog with my problem, but what else could I do?

"Chief Copegog, this thing I was telling you about, could you help me with it?"

"Could try, little girl, but I'm in spirit world now."

"Well, this problem is sort of *about* the spirit world."

He smiled, creasing up his already creased face.

"Okay, I help you then. Try, anyway."

So I told him about Kenny. And I made sure he knew that we, Kenny and I, were twins, just like his kids.

"And now," I finished up, "we —" I pointed to John and Noah — "we know for sure that Kenny is trying to talk to us from the spirit world but we don't know why or what he's trying to tell us.

"Could you," I blurted finally, "could you come with us and talk to him for me — I mean, us?"

Noah jabbed me in the ribs just as John hissed, "Are you *nuts*, Karen?"

Noah leaned over so that his mouth brushed against my ear and added so softly I could hardly pick up what he was saying, "It's the *same house*, remember? The house where he —"

"Sure," I said out loud, "but —"

"Karen," Noah whispered, "can you imagine what kind of forces would come pouring out of the next world if *he* came to your house?"

"Karen." It was John talking. "I think we better *talk* about this!"

Noah wouldn't let up. "Listen, don't you get it? If Chief Copegog comes to your house — and you conveniently left that little tidbit out when you asked your favour — don't you realize that Bond's ghost might join us too? Do you want them *both* in your upstairs hall? A murderer and a dirty rotten drunken cheat?"

I looked into the Chief's calm, sad face. I pushed Noah away and said to Chief Copegog, "Will you come?"

"Yep. Can't go 'way for too long, though." He pointed to the earth in front of him. "Think he's almost ready to cross over, and I got to be here when he's ready."

I got to my feet and said over John's and Noah's protests, "Let's go, then."

18

Tuesday Afternoon: Our House

Chief Copegog led the way back to the boat, with me behind him and the guys behind me. They talked excitedly to each other all the way but I couldn't make out what they were saying. And I was pretty sure I didn't *want* to know.

Chief Copegog sort of *glided* through the bush. The three of us were always shoving branches aside, ducking under things, waving mosquitoes away, tripping ourselves up. Not Chief Copegog. He hardly ever moved his arms. He slipped around and between trees like a — well, like a ghost. Except you could tell he had always walked that way.

The water in the bay was so calm and clear I could see the sand bottom and the trees that lined the shore were reflected on the surface.

John and Noah dragged the little aluminum boat from the trees and settled it into the calm water of the bay, breaking up the image of the sky and trees on the surface. Noah squatted and held the boat against the flat rock shore so we could get in. John dropped the packs into the bow of the boat where they thumped on the aluminum floor.

Chief Copegog stared down at the water behind the boat. The light breeze stirred his long black hair. A frown creased his brow and the corners of his mouth turned down.

"That boat, she don't smell so good."

I looked where Chief Copegog was looking. Around the scaly blue motor was a pretty rainbow floating on the water. Except I knew the rainbow was caused by gas and oil leaking into the lake.

"Sorry about that," said Noah. "It's my uncle's boat," he added, as if that explained anything.

I climbed into the boat, rocking it like crazy. Noah had to hold the gunwale to keep it steady. It wasn't a very big boat, and my weight made it tilt to one side.

I sat down on the centre seat, facing the back, then Chief Copegog stepped in, just like he would if he was stepping over a string that was lying on the ground. The boat didn't rock. It didn't even move. And after he sat down on the seat with me the boat still tilted to my side.

I shot a look at John. He made a soft whistling sound just before he scrambled into the back. Last came Noah, pushing off the rock beach as he hopped in. He plunked himself down beside John. The boat floated free.

I was shivering like mad and I could see John hugging himself to keep warm but pretending not to. The aluminum seat under me was like a slab of ice.

I turned to Chief Copegog and said as politely as I could, "Um . . . do you think you could turn down the cold a little?"

Chief Copegog looked startled for a second, then grinned, showing his stumpy teeth and the gaps where there weren't any.

"Can try, little girl."

The cold melted away. Most of it, anyway.

Noah pulled the choke on the old Evinrude, squeezed the bulb on the gas line, and then gave a great heave on the starter rope. The motor turned over a couple of times, coughing. A blue cloud of exhaust boiled out behind the boat. I looked at Chief Copegog. His eyes opened a little wider, then went back to normal. Then he scowled again and wrinkled his big flat nose.

"Scare all the ducks, birds, animals off with that stink and noise thing," he said. "Reminds me of that place, York."

Noah yanked again and the motor woke up, growling, then settled down to a drone.

As we turned out of the bay into the lake a long, sleek boat roared past. It was one of those speed boats we called cigarettes because they were so long and narrow and it was pulling four skiers on bright yellow ropes that fanned out from the back of the boat. The skiers came so close to us we could hear them laughing and screaming — three girls and a guy in black rubber wet suits — and the spray from the skis splashed us. They waved as they passed.

Chief Copegog grunted and looked around. It was still a sunny afternoon and there were lots of windsurfers out, trying to capture some of the light breeze in their wildly coloured sails. A cabin cruiser plowed down the channel, heading for the narrows, leaving a creamy wake behind it.

I wasn't paying too much attention to what was going on out on the lake, though. I was starting to feel pretty guilty about not telling Chief Copegog what house we lived in. Guilty and scared. What if Noah was right? What if, when Chief Copegog came into our house, he met up with Bond the Creep? And what if Noah was wrong? What if ghosts *could* hurt people?

Then another thought hit me. A thought that made me feel worse, not better. What if spirits could hurt other spirits? It sounded crazy, but it wasn't any crazier than droning across Lake Couchiching in an aluminum fishing boat with two boys and a ghost. What, I thought, if Bond's ghost hurt Chief Copegog?

And what if he hurt Kenny?

We were pretty near the town docks when I said to Noah, "How about you guys dropping Chief Copegog and me off at our boathouse."

I knew that Noah wouldn't want to leave the boat at our place because his uncle went fishing almost every night and he would be looking for his boat.

Noah spun the motor around and the boat swerved back up the lake.

"Sure, no problem."

I didn't want to say it out loud, but to get to our house from the town docks we'd have to walk through Couchiching Park, right past the big statue of Sammy Dee. I wasn't worried about people in the park seeing Chief Copegog. He could just not appear to them. I didn't want him to see the statue. I figured maybe he'd had enough of that stuff to last *ten* lifetimes.

When we got to our place I was relieved to see that Skinny Minnie wasn't in the back yard. Our house stood tall and silent, and the willow at the shore looked quiet and peaceful.

Noah cut the motor and the boat slipped neatly into the dark boathouse behind our rowboat. I scrambled up onto the dock and turned around to give Chief Copegog a hand.

He wasn't there.

"What the —"

"Look behind you, Karen." John was smiling, showing his braces to the world.

I turned to see Chief Copegog standing beside the rowboat. He wasn't laughing, though. He stood in the gloom of the boathouse quietly. He didn't look around or show any interest in where he was. Did he know, I wondered. His face was a grim, carved mask again — his mouth a hard straight line, eyes deep, like black caves.

"How did you *do* that?" I said.

His voice was like sandpaper dragged across metal. "Not so hard."

Noah restarted the motor, backed the boat out into the lake and headed toward the town docks. John waved to us.

I made up my mind then. I was going to tell Chief Copegog about our house.

"Chief Copegog, let's go sit in the sun, okay?" I said.

"Sure. Feel like a smoke too."

He didn't even look at our house when we stepped out into the sun. Squinting, I checked out the yard again to see if Minnie was there. She wasn't. I heard music — *Blonde Syrup*, her favourite group — coming from the front yard. She probably hadn't even *moved* since we left.

I led Chief Copegog to the dock and we sat at the end, our feet dangling, facing Chiefs' Island.

"Umm, Chief Copegog," I began.

He was unwrapping a cigar. Just before he stuck it into his mouth he said, "Yep, know that. Recognized it right away." He laid the cellophane wrapper on the plank beside him.

"You . . . you read my mind!"

He struck a match from a matchbook that said *Champlain Hotel* on it and held the match to the tip of the cigar. He puffed a few times, jetting thick white smoke out of his mouth. He squeezed the burned match head to powder and placed the match on the plank beside the wrapper. He took the cigar out of his mouth, looked at it, then at me.

"I get pictures sometimes, what you're thinkin'."

"Is that how you knew . . . um, is that why you told me that night you knew I had troubles?"

He nodded and looked out over the green lake. He looked the same way he did in the graveyard when he stared off into the trees. The afternoon sun was bright on the shore of Chiefs' Island. Chief Copegog pointed back over his shoulder with his thumb, back to our house.

"Looks better now, that house. Got a good feelin' comin' from it, mostly."

I didn't catch on to that "mostly" at first. I was too busy feeling relieved.

"Are you . . . are you sorry you . . . about what happened between you and Bond?"

Chief Copegog was silent for a moment before

he answered. "Killin', that's never no good. He was bad man, that Bond. But I met lots of bad mens all the time I been alive. Some white mens, some my peoples. Can't go 'round killin' all them mens you think is bad. But that time, I lost my smart thinkin'."

He touched himself on his chest. "Thought with my heart. Kilt him for my family reasons."

Chief Copegog heaved a big sigh. "Nope," he said again, "killin', that's never no good."

I looked down into the still water at my feet. I could see a school of minnows darting around, back and forth. A water spider skated across the surface, a dimple under each of his legs where it rested on the water.

"I wouldn't blame you if you decided to change your mind about helping me and Kenny, Chief Copegog. I mean, now that you know where we live. This place must hold really bad memories for you. Noah thinks that Bond the Cr — that Bond's spirit might be there, as well as Kenny's."

Chief Copegog took a drag on the cigar and let the smoke roll out his nostrils. With his other hand he pulled at his earlobe.

His voice had a hard edge to it. "Know he's there," he said slowly. "Can feel him."

I felt a pain like somebody just punched me in the stomach. A fear pain. Except fear isn't a strong enough word. Now I knew why, a couple of minutes ago, he had said "mostly."

I turned and looked at the house. It was shadowed now and the windows stared out across the yard at me like blank lifeless eyes. Suddenly it didn't look like the home I loved. It looked like an enemy.

Bond's ghost was in there.

"Is Kenny in there, too?" I asked Chief Copegog. "Can you feel him?"

"Could feel him when we was out on the water. Yep, he's around here all right."

"Is he . . . do you think Bond would hurt him?"

"Don't know 'bout that, little girl. My peoples, once they're on the Other Side, they can't hurt each other. But we're all between worlds now. And the Whites, they're strange peoples. Don't know about them."

It sounded strange, him talking like that. I mean, I was a White, but he never seemed to include me when he talked about them.

"Do you have any idea why Kenny is in our house?"

"He wants talk to you. You're his born same minute sister. That Bond, I dunno why he's here. Maybe trapped between Sides, like me."

I wished he'd quit talking about Bond. I didn't really care about him. He scared the life out of me and I wished he'd go wherever he was supposed to be. But all I cared about was getting Kenny back.

"I wonder why Kenny is in between Sides," I said.

A shadow of surprise crossed Chief Copegog's face.

"Thought you maybe knew that," he said. "It's you. You're keepin' him here."

About fifteen minutes later John and Noah came walking across the yard. They came over to the dock. Chief Copegog had finished his cigar and was sitting staring out over the lake. He could do that, I learned — sit and say nothing and stare. I wondered what he was thinking. Was he scared, as scared as I was? Was he sad?

"Well," John said, "guess we should go in."

We walked across the yard and went into the kitchen.

"Let's go upstairs, Chief Copegog," I said.

And that's when we heard it.

It was as if the house had been holding its breath. Waiting. As soon as Chief Copegog was inside it breathed out slowly in a long, long sigh, the way you do when you've been expecting something bad to happen and it finally comes along. Only this was worse. Lots worse. It sounded like hate. And fear. It made my skin crawl.

"What the heck was *that*?" John exclaimed from behind me.

The long wicked sigh sighed again, like a curse.

Noah said, "I don't like the sound of it, whatever it was."

"That's spirit world talkin'," Chief Copegog said.

Our feet thumped faster on the stairs. The closer we got to the top, the colder we felt. As soon as we got into the upstairs hall and turned toward my room the sigh changed to deep, fast, loud breathing. Like something chasing you in a nightmare.

Bam! Bam! Bam! One by one, all the bedroom doors slammed shut.

I looked at Chief Copegog. He didn't seem as scared as I was. He didn't seem scared at all. But his face was hard and dark and grim.

He led the way down the hall to my room and opened the door. He went inside.

We followed him. Before I got to the door I stopped and looked at the floor.

There was a large, dark brown stain on the hardwood. It filled the space in front of my door.

"What's that?" I said, afraid to know.

"It looks like —" John began. His voice was shaking so badly I could hardly understand him.

Noah's vocal cords weren't working so hot either.

"Yeah, it's a blood stain," he croaked.

The heavy breathing sound began again, deep long breaths, as if the hallway was a throat. The sound rose, getting louder and louder, until it was like a roaring wind.

We rushed into my room, stepping over the blood, and slammed the door behind us.

19

Tuesday Afternoon: My Room

I was the last one into the room so I locked the door and leaned against it, panting. Chief Copegog looked around and walked over to my desk. He pushed the lamp aside and climbed up on top, sitting there cross-legged and rigid. John sat on the windowsill and Noah pulled up the desk chair. I lowered myself onto the waterbed. We formed a sort of circle.

No one said anything. The roaring out in the hall suddenly stopped dead.

I heaved a big sigh and looked around. I could see past John out the window. The late afternoon sun lit up Chiefs' Island and the far shore of Lake Couchiching. My eyes focused on John's face. It was pale and he was chewing on his lower lip. Noah didn't look too confident either. He kept fidgeting with his earring. I could hear the silver cross tap, tap, tap against his thumbnail. Chief Copegog stared straight ahead as if he was looking through the wall. I wondered what he was seeing.

It was warmer in the room than in the hall, but still chilly. I was hanging on hard to control myself. It felt as if the house was filled with some kind of *weight* — like when you're worried bad about something it weighs you down and when you move, your arms and legs feel heavy. And inside my mind, hopes and fears spun around each other so fast I was starting to lose control like I did after Kenny died.

Even though I was cold and confused and more scared than I had ever been in my life, a strange thought slipped into my head. In the hall the ghost of a murdered man was making doors slam and bleeding on the floor and roaring, and there inside my room another ghost was perched on my desk — but outside it was a warm sunny day. It was all wrong. There should have been thunder and lightning and wind that tossed the wet branches, making them scrape against the windows, like in books. I almost laughed. I almost cried.

My eye was caught by the hook on my closet door. It hung down uselessly.

"Chief Copegog," I said, but my voice cracked and I had to start again. "Chief Copegog, is Kenny in there?" I pointed to the closet.

"Nope. Can't feel him anywhere this house."

I felt disappointed and relieved at the same time. The thing in the house wouldn't hurt him. But where *was* he?

Just then the house breathed again — different this time but just as terrifying. Instead of a sigh it was like a long, tired groan. It went on and on. John's eyes bugged out and his knuckles went white as he squeezed the edge of the windowsill. Noah stopped tapping the cross with his thumbnail and linked his fingers together in his lap to make one tight fist.

We waited for Chief Copegog to do something, but he kept staring at the wall. His face was even more mask-like and wooden than usual. He seemed off in his own world. If he was, I didn't blame him.

The groaning got louder, sort of seeping from the walls and ceilings. The groans were separated now, long and painful and angry, like a man was lifting something heavy, so heavy it hurt him.

I stared at my door. There was something outside in the hall. I looked at the wind chimes. Nothing.

"What's that dragging noise?" John's voice trembled.

Noah moved his head back and forth, slowly. His lips were pressed together. I bet he wished he'd never read a ghost book in his life, I thought.

The dragging noise continued along with the painful groaning. And it was getting louder.

Someone was dragging himself toward my room.

"It's him," Noah said finally. "It has to be."

He didn't have to say who he meant.

All three of us stared at Chief Copegog as if we had realized at the same moment that it was his move next. His face was like a dark painting — no movement, not even a hint that anything was going on around him. Outside the room the groans got louder and louder and seemed to pound inside my skull. The dragging was a man pulling himself in agony along the floor — drag, pause, drag — a man drowning in pain.

I knew I was going to go crazy if somebody didn't do something. I opened my mouth but didn't get the chance to say anything.

Chief Copegog blinked. And with the blink his face came alive, as if he had been asleep all this time. His features seemed to sag. His wrinkles were like lines of pain across his face.

He nodded to himself and, a moment later, unfolded his legs and slid from the desk. He took a deep breath and began to walk toward the door.

"Chief Copegog, what are you going to —"

"Don't open the door!" I cut John's question off.

But it was too late. The door slowly opened.

Chief Copegog stood between me and the horrible thing in the hallway, but it was as if I could see *through* him. My arm raised itself, pointing into the hall.

"Look," my voice said.

John stood and crept slowly toward me and gripped my hand so tight it hurt. He craned his neck to see out the bedroom door. Noah stood up slowly from his chair and moved toward me too, until his shoulder touched mine. The three of us stared at the thing we had feared would be there.

The man in the hallway lay on the floor, one arm stretched toward us, the hand on the end like a claw scratching at the wood. He raised himself a little, groaning, then dragged himself along the floor with his outstretched arm, then dropped to the floor with a painful grunt. He struggled toward us, little by little. But Chief Copegog blocked the way.

Bond's face was terrifying — as white as flour, twisted with pain and anger and hate. He stared ahead of him out of bright colourless eyes that cut into you like razors. His black hair was long and stringy.

We could see now that his other hand was clutching a long-handled knife that stuck out of his chest.

Around his hand his shirt was soaked with blood that left a long ugly smear down the hallway. Bond was dressed in a long black coat and dark grey pants with pinstripes. His shirt was white at the neck with a high collar and one of those old-fashioned ties. The big diamond pin in the tie sparkled in a grisly background of blood.

He hauled himself forward again, coughing from deep down, and bright red blood ran out of his mouth. It dripped off the end of his chin onto the floor.

He raised his head higher and those razor-eyes caught sight of Chief Copegog.

Oh, oh, I thought. I gulped, and realized I had been holding my breath. John's grip on my right hand tightened. I heard Noah catch his breath. We waited.

The feelings that twisted the man's face into a knot of hate and pain must have changed, because his face went blank. Instantly. Then his eyebrows raised, like he was asking a question.

After a moment Chief Copegog nodded.

"What's going on?" John asked. "What's happening?"

Noah's face was strangely calm. "I think we're going to see an old, old crime being rubbed out. I *think*. We *could* be watching —"

"Shhhhhh!" I hissed. "Look!"

Chief Copegog leaned over. He gripped the knife — his knife — by the handle. He drew the knife slowly out of Bond's chest.

"Oh, God!" John moaned as a gush of bright blood rushed out of the wound as the long blade came away.

Chief Copegog stood up straight, blood dripping from the blade of his knife. He stared at the knife for a moment.

Then he dropped it.

Bond's wide eyes followed the knife as it fell in slow motion to the floor and hit the wood soundlessly. It bounced, flicking droplets of blood into the air, then lay still. Bond looked up at Chief Copegog again. Chief Copegog's eyes moved from the knife to Bond and the eyes of the two men locked, like lasers coming at one another, locked on the same path. Both men were still, quiet, as if they were talking to each other along those laser beams, as if they didn't need to use voices anymore, not after all these years.

All my fear disappeared in a flash and I felt suddenly very sad as I watched those two men staring at each other after a hundred and fifty years of wandering alone between two worlds. Bond must have been caught between two worlds just like Chief Copegog.

Noah must have been thinking what I was thinking. "This is it," was all he said.

"What is what?" John asked, irritated.

"Chief Copegog has to forgive him," Noah added. "Bond has to be forgiven by the guy he harmed, see? Because he used Chief Copegog to cheat the Ojibways out of their land. Yeah," Noah was getting excited, the way you do when you solve some kind of problem, when everything suddenly gets clear, "and Chief Copegog has to be forgiven by Bond for killing him."

"Why should anyone forgive *Bond*?" John said.

"Come on, John," Noah said. "Bond paid. Take a look at him."

John said, "Yeah, I guess you're right. Look at that blood."

Bond and Chief Copegog were still locked in on each other — a man in an old-fashioned formal suit with leather shoes and a diamond stick-pin in his tie and a guy with long hair, dressed in skins.

Then, slowly, each one of them nodded.

Bond slowly raised himself to his knees, then to his feet. As he stood, the blood that stained his shirt and coat gradually disappeared as if it was seeping back into his body.

Then Bond did a strange thing. He straightened his tie and buttoned his jacket as if he was expecting company and had just heard the doorbell ring. He turned without a sound and walked silently, floated, almost, down the hall. When he got to the top of the stairs he disappeared. He was there, then he wasn't.

Chief Copegog turned and walked into my room. It might have been my imagination but I thought his shoulders didn't look so slumped and the lines in his face didn't seem so rigid.

Noah was staring down at the floor. He raised his arm and pointed.

"Look," he said quietly.

The blood was gone.

Tuesday Afternoon: Chief Copegog

The four of us stood in the doorway of my room, staring at the spot where Bond had disappeared a moment before.

I said to Chief Copegog, "Where did he go?"

"He's goin' to Other Side now."

"I gotta sit down," John moaned. "I think I'm gonna faint."

Noah sat down on the desk chair again. John flopped full length onto my waterbed and rocked up and down for a second. I was about to ask Chief Copegog about Kenny when Noah began to talk.

"Chief Copegog, how come Bond can go to the Other Side and you're still here? I don't think that's fair. We know what a bad man he was. You weren't — I mean, aren't. I don't get it."

I felt suddenly ashamed when he said that. I had been thinking about me and my twin brother. I had forgotten all about Chief Copegog. Here he was helping me and I was ignoring him.

"Not worry, little girl," he said. He had read my mind again.

He turned to me and smiled. "Now I got somethin' to say to all you kids, specially Karen."

Behind me I could hear John sloshing the waterbed, so he must have sat up.

Chief Copegog walked to the window. He turned slowly and stood there, his thick arms folded across his broad chest. It was strange, but he looked taller. He stood straight, with his shoulders back. He looked strong — not like an old man at all. I thought this must have been how he looked before he died — old, but powerful and straight.

"Hear my words, what I'm sayin'," he began. His voice sounded firm and very formal, and there was rhythm in his talk, like when he told us about his family. The S's in his words whispered and whistled.

"Your peoples, the Whites, they think, somethin's real, they got to be able to touch it, hold it in their hands. But lotta things — love, joy, hope — you can't hold them things in your hand. But them things, they're alive, they're real, like the red and gold on the hills in the autumn and the sound of the breeze when it sings in the marsh grasses.

"You kids, you thought Kenny was gone 'cause he got kilt out there on the road. You figured, couldn't see him no more, couldn't touch him, couldn't hear him laugh, he was gone forever. Now you know, that's the wrong thinkin'. Spirit world is all around us, like the air. I tol' you that. I tell you again, now. Hear my words, what I'm sayin'. Spirit world is *alive*."

Chief Copegog looked directly at me. His eyes weren't fierce now, but they sure were serious.

"Karen, you let that wrong thinkin' hurt you bad. You thought Kenny, he was gone forever. That's why your mind ran away from his dyin'. You hid your face from his dyin', tried to pretend it never happened. That wrong thinkin', it tore you down, made you small inside. Now you got to *believe* in Kenny. You got to let your dead brother help you, make you strong. Because he's real. He's still livin' in your memory" — he touched his forehead, then his chest with the flat of his hand — "in your heart. He ain't never goin' to leave them places. Let him make you *strong*."

Chief Copegog crossed his arms again.

"That's what I wanted to say."

Chief Copegog stopped talking. I could hear John behind me. He was making that sniffling noise he made when he cried but tried to hide it. I looked at Noah. He swallowed hard. Me, I was crying too, quietly. I didn't think I'd have any tears left after what had happened in the last few days, but I could feel them hot on my cheeks. They itched a little.

I knew, I knew what Chief Copegog was saying was true. I had been selfish. But . . .

"It's just that . . . that there's a big empty hole inside me since Kenny . . . went away."

I felt an arm around my shoulder. It was John. "Didn't you listen to what he said, Karen? Kenny *didn't* go away. Not *really*."

I turned to my brother and pressed my face to his bony chest. "But it *hurts*!" I cried. "I miss him!"

I heard Chief Copegog's voice behind me. "You got to let Kenny help you," he said again. "You got to let him make you strong."

I lifted my head up. John's arms were still around me. I nodded, and tried to wipe the tears away from my face.

"I wish I could talk to him, or at least see him," I whispered.

"You can," said Chief Copegog. "He's down there."

He turned and pointed out the window, down into the yard. I burst from John's arms and ran to look through the glass, knowing all of a sudden where he would be.

I was right. Although it was sunny in the yard, the willow tree glowed as if it was a lampshade and inside it was a million-watt bulb.

Tuesday Afternoon: The Willow

"**C**ome on!" I shouted as I shot to the bedroom door.

I ran down the back stairs and through the kitchen and out the back door. John and Noah stumbled and banged along right behind me. I dashed across the back lawn to the willow tree, but when I got there I stopped short.

It was hot in the yard, even though the sun was behind the house. It was still too, not even a hint of a breeze. The willow branches hung straight and quiet. Behind them, I could see — *feel* — the bright white light.

And I could see the shape of someone in there, sitting on the big branch.

"Wow," breathed John when he caught up to me.

"Is he in there?" asked Noah, puffing.

"Yes," I answered. My heart was pounding so hard I could hardly squeeze the word out. I swallowed on a dry throat.

"Are you coming in with me, John?" I asked, not taking my eyes from the tree.

"Uh, I don't think so," John said quietly. "I think it's you he wants to see, Karen."

"Besides," he said, his voice breaking, "to tell you the truth, I don't think I could take it."

"Okay, John, I know what you mean."

I looked at Noah. "Wish me luck," I said.

"Luck, Karen. And listen, remember what Chief Copegog said, okay?"

I stepped forward slowly. As I got close to the willow everything seemed to *magnify* — I mean, all my senses seemed to magnify what was coming in. The grass whispered around the soles of my Nikes. The air got cold, and seemed to lie against my skin like a damp cloth. I reached out and parted the willow branches like a curtain. The leaves scraped my skin as I stepped into the special place that Kenny and I always thought of as our very own.

The light was terrifically bright, but it didn't hurt my eyes and I could still see everything — every leaf, every twist of the old tree's bark — clearer than I ever saw it before.

It was Kenny all right. You couldn't miss the wild red hair, the freckles, the devilish look in his eyes. He sat on the branch, legs dangling like he'd been resting there relaxed until I showed up. He was wearing his skating clothes. His helmet was gone, one knee pad was missing and his shirt was torn a little.

He doesn't look bad for a kid who's been run over, I thought. In fact, he's just about the sweetest-looking little boy there is.

And that's when it hit me.

Little boy.

It hit me so hard I sucked in my breath and my knees got watery and I had to lean on the trunk of the willow to steady myself.

Little boy. Kenny didn't look exactly like me anymore! He was a — a child! His face and his arms were plump. I knew that if he got down from the branch and stood in front of me he'd only come up to my shoulder.

Little boy. He was two years younger than I was! I had kept growing in the past two years, but Kenny had stopped. Ever since, I thought.

Ever since he died.

And then everything got clear.

Everything that Chief Copegog had tried to tell me got suddenly clear. Like when I looked through Dad's binoculars and things were blurry at first. Everything was *there* — I could tell what I was looking at. The shapes were there. But when I turned the eye pieces all of a sudden the shapes became *things* — clear and bright.

Little boy.

I could feel the tears coming again, cool on my cheeks. It was *me*. I had been keeping Kenny between the two worlds for two whole years. I knew what Chief Copegog had meant now. And I knew what Kenny wanted to tell me.

Kenny smiled then. *I'm okay.*

The thought slipped into my mind and I knew that it came from Kenny.

I could feel a big weight slowly lifting from me. *I understand, now, Kenny*, I thought to him. *I'm sorry*, I added. *I didn't realize*.

He shook his head the way he used to do to say, that's okay. No problem.

I took a deep breath. *I'll be all right*, I thought to him. *I want you to go to the Other Side*.

I felt a question in my mind.

Yes, I mean it, Kenny. It's time. I know that now.

Kenny grinned again, making his freckles dance. He nodded.

I didn't want to go back out from under the willow to the yard, but I knew I had to. Kenny would stay as long as I wanted. So I had to leave first.

Good-bye, Kenny, I thought to him. *I — we all— love you*.

My twin brother raised his hand in farewell. There was a scrape on his palm, and a smudge of dirt.

I turned and parted the branches and stepped into the yard.

Tuesday Afternoon: Ending

The warm air of the yard closed around me.
"Well?" John said, his voice trembling.
"It's okay," I said. "Everything is okay."
"Yep, thought you'd say that."

Chief Copegog! He was standing on the lawn by the kitchen door. There was a big smile on his face — a smile with black squares where the teeth were missing.

The three of us walked up to him. I didn't know what to say. John didn't either, I guess, although that was hard to believe. Anyway, he kept quiet.

"What a day this has been!" Noah said, shaking his head. "Unbelievable!"

"Might be I better go now," Chief Copegog said, pulling his earlobe.

"Hey, wait a minute!" I jumped in.

Then I shut up. You're doing it again, Karen,